"Strip."

"I beg your pardon?" Her shock erupted as a nervous laugh.

The same cute sound, from early that morning, that had been so damn attractive. *Stow it, Marine.* One more time, he debated sharing why it was important to wait on the supplies he needed. He'd be prepared this time.

"I'll wash your clothes while you shower. How did you think we were going to clean up?"

"I... That can't possibly be a good idea—what if they come here and I'm—"

"Soapy?" He laughed, unable to stop himself. The look on her face was priceless. "We weren't followed. Promise. If you're worried about getting on the road, you should probably get moving."

She stood and Dallas jumped off the couch to follow. Bree picked her up and Jake held out his hands to take her.

"The paramedics warned me about an infection." He pointed to his bullet graze. "Do it for me. After all, I did save your life."

THE MARINE'S LAST DEFENSE

—

Angi Morgan

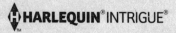

HARLEQUIN® INTRIGUE®

Recycling programs for this product may not exist in your area.

Dallas and Valentine—two sweet puppies who gave love every minute they were here. THANKS, Steve, for your quick responses to my many questions and your many years of service as a police officer. AND THANKS, Jen—we both know this book wouldn't have happened without you.

ISBN-13: 978-0-373-69738-0

THE MARINE'S LAST DEFENSE

Copyright © 2014 by Angela Platt

Printed in U.S.A.

www.Harlequin.com

ABOUT THE AUTHOR

Angi Morgan writes Harlequin Intrigue novels "where honor and danger collide with love." She combines actual Texas settings with characters who are in realistic and dangerous situations. Angi has been a finalist for the Bookseller's Best Award, *RT Book Reviews* Best First Series, Gayle Wilson Award of Excellence and the Daphne du Maurier Award.

Angi and her husband live in North Texas, with only the four-legged "kids" left in the house to interrupt her writing. They recently began volunteering for a local Labrador foster program. Visit her website, www.angimorgan.com, or hang out with her on Facebook.

Books by Angi Morgan

HARLEQUIN INTRIGUE
1232—HILL COUNTRY HOLDUP
1262—.38 CALIBER COVER-UP
1406—DANGEROUS MEMORIES
1423—PROTECTING THEIR CHILD
1471—THE MARINE'S LAST DEFENSE

CAST OF CHARACTERS

Detective Jake Craig—Former marine and military cop, now a D.P.D. homicide detective. Divorced when he left the military, he hasn't allowed himself to connect with people—especially the officers who resent his recent promotion. But something about a gal in a coffee shop gets him thinking that might all change.

Sabrina Watkins—She's always preferred four-legged friends, and grew a dog-walking service into a successful pet-boarding business. Can she keep herself from growing attached to the handsome and broody detective who's trying to arrest her?

Griffin Tyler—Veterinarian, Kate's partner and her childhood friend who has many secrets of his own.

Detective Elton Owens—Jake's partner, who leads the resentment of Jake's recent promotion to homicide detective.

Helen Richardson—Murdered. She recently rescued a puppy from the shelter. Could the Labrador have anything to do with her death?

Uncle Jerry—The only family member who knows Sabrina's secret. Can Jake and Sabrina find him before the murderer?

Dallas—A bounding fifty-pound six-month-old solid-black Labrador. Abandoned as a puppy, blind in one eye, sassy and adopted by Helen Richardson.

Prologue

Six Months Ago

"Keep the girl alive. I'm telling you it would be less complicated," Griffin Tyler said. "More money for us, too."

"You don't tell us nothin', Tyler."

Sabrina Watkins flattened herself to the hall paneling. *They wanted to kill her?* She'd been three years behind Griffin in high school, been in youth group with this man who had become her business partner. And recently she'd thought of him as a very close friend. Their mothers even still went to the same church every Sunday morning.

"She has too many friends," the unknown voice continued. "Too many that will believe her when she claims she's innocent. If we leave her alive to chat 'em up, everybody gets sympathetic. It's better to kill her. Make it look like a suicide and then evidence comes out proving how guilty she is. We lose a little money framing her, but overall the operation survives. You set up shop somewhere else. Insurance, no one's the wiser."

She didn't know the second voice. Average tone, not deep or high. She didn't think he'd ever boarded a pet with her. She'd only seen the back of the man's head as she'd rounded the corner from the offices into the clinic. She had no description for the police and didn't even know his hair color since he was wearing a ball cap.

"Whatever," Griffin said, not trying hard to sway his partner. "Suicide works. She's surrounded herself with the business for the past two years. Everything she has is tied up in it. When it goes up in flames, our hometown will think she was too depressed to start over." He put his hands on his hips, a gesture she'd seen a thousand times when he was ready to move on from a subject. "When will you do it?"

Oh, my Lord, they really are going to kill me, she thought, panicking. *Why? What did I do?*

"Listen, Tyler, you're the one who screwed up. Too many fingers in the pie. You should never have involved the local cop who's getting greedy. The higher-ups want them both gone, along with all traces of the connection to us. You're damn lucky they don't want you gone."

Who have you gotten involved with, Griffin?

Sabrina's heart pounded faster than Tweetiepie, the miniature Chihuahua she'd groomed at the truck stop that afternoon. Her hands shook even while she was plastered against the wall. She wanted to close her eyes and have someone explain why this was happening. Could someone wake her up from this nightmare so she could go back to her simple life of boarding pets?

Her thoughts drifted through her last conversation with Griffin. As far as she knew there had been no indicators that he was upset with her. But, then again, how did your best friend speak to you three hours before casually mentioning no one would miss you if you were dead?

Wait. Flames? Had he said flames?

Was Griffin speaking in metaphors or were they really going to burn the clinic down? "Gone…all traces." She had to get to the police. No. The stranger had mentioned involving a cop. Which one? They didn't mention anyone by name. Who could she trust? But they couldn't all be bad. Right?

What could she tell them if she did trust them? She'd overheard her business partner plotting to kill a "she," but unfortunately there were a lot of "shes" in Amarillo, Texas.

She'd look like an idiot. Griffin continued his discussion with the stranger. She couldn't distinguish their words as they walked to the rear exit. She dropped to the floor and crept around the corner into the operating room.

Griffin was right about one thing—she had no other life outside the clinic or pet sitting. He was also right that every dime she had was tied up in her half of the business.

But right now, she needed help.

No one worked in the clinic on Sundays. She made a special trip with the house-call van once a month, working with truck drivers. It was five o'clock and she'd spent the afternoon grooming dogs at the I-40 truck stop and let Amber borrow her car for a baby shower. If she hadn't finished an hour early, decided to restock the van while waiting on her assistant's return, she wouldn't have a clue about their plot to kill her and burn the clinic.

She'd been so dumb. Well, not anymore. It was time to get closer, find out what they were doing.

On her hands and knees, she scooted across the painted concrete floor. Staying close to the counters and then behind the stainless steel exam table, she was careful not to knock any of the rolling trays full of instruments. She'd never felt comfortable in this room. It wasn't organized and certainly didn't function effectively according to what she'd seen over the past two years.

There were many times she'd wondered how Griffin made any money. Now she knew. He made it illegally. She dared to look around the side of the table. There wasn't enough light in her section of the room for her to be seen, but she was still very careful.

"So we're agreed. Tonight," the stranger said. "Get your cop friend to patrol nearby. I'll nab the girl before the fire's set and make it look real enough."

"You think it's necessary to burn the place with the animals inside?"

"You want the fire to look genuine, don't ya?"

The stranger was near the back door. She caught a tilt to his lips when Griffin's back was turned. Her stomach twisted in fear. Whoever this stranger was, he enjoyed killing. Animal or human, that smile indicated he looked forward to it.

She swallowed the bile in her throat and hid behind the island table again. *Oh, God. Oh, God. Oh, God. They were going to kill her.*

What should she do? Remember his voice. Remember that deadly smile and his thin, flat lips. She had no evidence, no proof that someone wanted her dead. And from what she'd overheard, they'd planted evidence that she was responsible for something. Dear Lord, she didn't even know where to start. She knew nothing about police procedures except that they needed more information than she had to begin an investigation.

Fading daylight briefly filled the room as the back door opened and closed. The sound of the dead bolt turning echoed through the cold room. Oh, no, the van was parked out front now. How long had they been here? Would they notice? Would they come back?

Silence.

She sank to the floor. There was nowhere to hide and if they did return, what could she do?

The faint whine of an abandoned pup bolted her into action. No one was going to kill the animals left in her care. She tugged on one of the rolling tables and opened a bin. She yanked a scalpel, wielding it like a hunting knife. She could defend herself a little, maybe deter them long enough to race out the front door.

Explanation or no, she could get to the police to save her own life. Panda and Pogo barked.

The animals. She had to get them out of the building. She took a peek through the windows and didn't see any cars. She ran through the clinic to the back of the boarding kennels and unbolted the door, slightly propping it open for quick access. Then another dash through the building and out the front, moving the van to the back.

Thank goodness she didn't have a lot of animals at the clinic or being boarded for the weekend. The three dogs and kitty would fit inside the van and be safe. She closed the van door with a sigh of relief, dropping her forehead to the cooling metal. She could meet Amber at the house and have her drive the animals to their owners.

Then she would drive her car directly to the police station and take her chances. Crazy sounding or not, she had to report Griffin to the authorities.

"Back early?"

She yelped like one of the puppies. "Oh, Griffin. You scared the living daylights out of me." Her partner jerked her away from the van in a constricted grip. "You're hurting me."

"Don't play dumb, Sabrina. I saw you loading the animals. You heard us inside and are moving them before we torch the place."

She pulled. His grip tightened. "I don't understand any of this, Griffin. What's going on?"

"Get inside." He shoved a gun in her ribs. "Now."

"Don't do this. Don't kill me, please. Whatever the problem is we can work it out." She stumbled as he propelled her through the door. "I'm sure the police can sort through everything."

"No, they can't. I don't give the orders. I follow them. My office."

The gun was securely in his hand and she shuffled through the kennels sideways, unwilling to turn her back to him. What if he had the same maniacal smile as the stranger?

Had Griffin shot someone before? He couldn't have. He wasn't the man who drowned kittens—he was the veterinarian who saved them. Right? But he was an excellent marksman, who wouldn't miss when he fired.

How am I ever going to get away from you? she wondered.

"Is it drugs? Money laundering? Who are you working for?" she asked, stalling. *Think, think, think.* She couldn't allow herself to be trapped in his office. There was no way out. Only a slit of a window, high above her head.

"None of the whys or whos matter anymore, Sabrina. There's nothing you can do."

"Doing nothing is exactly what I did for the past two years while you plotted to set me up to commit suicide." She stopped at his office door, so close to her own.

Unfortunately, her box of an office would be just as bad as his. The window was just as high. There weren't any weapons inside. The can of pepper spray her father insisted she carry was on her key chain, in the van. Her only path out of the building was blocked by Griffin.

"I didn't think they'd really kill anybody. You were supposed to take the blame, but they never said they'd kill you. But it's you or me and I won't let it be me. I'm lucky I came back for my *insurance* before they torch this place. Otherwise, we'd both be dead by morning."

The light in his office was already on. The door was ajar

enough to see an open briefcase overstuffed with paper. His insurance?

"I can't believe you're going to just kill me." But she knew he meant what he said. What if *she* got his "insurance"?

Tears of fear trickled down her cheeks. She covered her face with her hands, leaning close to the picture of puppies they'd rescued last year. But she wouldn't voluntarily move another inch to her death so she spread her feet for a stronger fighting position.

He'd relaxed, leaned lazily against her office door. If she could just delay him long enough to grab the briefcase and get to the van…she might have a chance.

"It's no use," he said. "You might as well stop stalling."

Sabrina looked up, plucking the scalpel from her pocket. "Would you stop?" she shouted, lunging at his leg, stabbing him as deeply as she could.

He screamed. Fell. The gun went off. She darted into his office, grabbed his briefcase of "insurance" and ran for her life.

Chapter One

"I didn't complain when I was a private. I didn't complain while serving three tours in Afghanistan. These guys have no clue how to make life miserable for someone like me. I can take a few icy sidewalks and midnight shifts."

Jake Craig skidded on the slushy cement. Digging his steel-toed boots into the ice, he balanced on the slippery incline before he embarrassed himself by slamming to the ground. His partner—sitting in the nice warm car—probably had his smartphone ready, just waiting for him to fall flat on his butt so he could record it all.

The cold of the early morning felt good compared to the many long, hot desert memories he had from six years of war. North Texas cold didn't compare to the bitter mountain freezing when he thought he'd lose his toes. Yeah, he could take his turn walking in the cold. At least this time he didn't have seventy pounds of gear to carry.

On the Dallas P.D. a little over a year, he'd recently transferred to the homicide division. The promotion raised more than a few eyebrows when he jumped from rookie to detective—skipping everything in between, including the right to do so. Not too amazing for former military personnel. His fellow P.D. officers knew about department politics where qualified ex-military got bumped to the head of the list. It didn't keep them from resenting him or make being the butt of their jokes any easier.

Just like now when he'd been directed to search for a dead body. An anonymous 911 call claimed there was a dead woman at the lake moving around in the bushes. He'd asked dispatch to repeat and again the claim was that a dead woman was moving around in the bushes.

"You go see if you can find that ghost," his partner had ordered when they'd arrived. He'd leaned his head against the headrest and shut his eyes. "I'm going to keep the heater running on these old bones, *partner*. You love the cold, don't cha, *partner?*"

"Sure, Owens. I could stay out here all freakin' day." Okay, maybe his reply had been a slight exaggeration. Then again, he hadn't actually replied, just mumbled after he'd left the car. He would continue to accept the late shifts, practical jokes and crank calls, just like he had this morning.

"I'm a freakin' machine." No one could break down the machine at work.

The ghost was probably a drunk trying to get out of the snowfall, but it had to be checked out. What if the call was just a staged joke? Could Owens have arranged for a "ghost" to be at the spillway?

It was the perfect setup. Someone could pop out of the bushes, try to surprise him, and he might even lose his footing. "I will not fall and have that humiliation blasted across the internet. I'll never hear the end of it." Those guys knew he'd be the one out here verifying ghosts don't exist. And he wouldn't put it past any of them to have cooked up this entire charade.

As long as they dished it out, he'd take it. The cold,

searching for a ghost, whatever, he'd keep at the job. He wanted the job. He had nothing else but the job. He wouldn't let it slip through his fingers like the rest of his life.

An early morning search of the underbrush around White Rock Lake beat picking up Friday-night drunks from Deep Ellum any night of the week. Homicide detectives wore civilian clothes, a definite improvement from the street cops. Man, he was glad to be out of a uniform. Any uniform.

His years as a marine MP didn't seem to make a difference to his coworkers. Maybe they thought he was more qualified to deal with drunks than legitimate homicides. If they only knew what he wanted to forget.

The beam from the flashlight reflected off a pair of red eyes. The animal didn't bolt. Jake took a step closer to the fence and heard the low whine of a dog.

A black Labrador was under the brush on the other side of the six-foot security fence. Located just below a large yellow-and-orange danger sign, warning that the lake's spillway was nearby.

The leash must have tangled around a limb, pinning the dog to the cold February ground. The pup yelped, whining louder, visibly shaking from the cold. He dropped back to the ground, obviously tired from his struggle for freedom.

"Hang on, now. How'd you get over there?" Just to his right the section of fence was raised off the ground, easy enough for a dog or person to crawl under.

Jake clicked off the light and dropped it in his pocket. Going over the icy fence was a lot cleaner than crawling under like the dog had. He shook the chain-link fence, verifying it could hold his weight, and scaled it in a few seconds, landing on the spillway side with both feet firm in the melting snow.

"So you're the ghost those drunks reported?" He knelt and offered his hand for the Lab to sniff. It quickly licked his fingers. "You're friendly enough. What are you caught on?"

The stubborn dog refused to budge even with encouragement and a gentle tug on his collar. His young bark did some tugging of its own on Jake's heart—he hadn't thought he had one left—earning a smile from a jaded soldier.

He pushed farther into the bushes, conceding that the only way to get the dog loose was to get wet himself. The poor mutt shivered hard enough to knock his tags together. Jake could relate, having been there a time or two.

Working his tall frame closer, his slacks were soaked as the slush seeped through the cloth. The snow that dropped on the back of his neck quickly melted from his body heat and dampened his skin. He slipped his hand around the dog collar and tugged again, receiving a louder howl and whimper.

"Are you hurt, boy? Is that why you can't move? All right, then. I might as well send my coat to the cleaners, too." He stretched onto his belly, sliding forward until he could reach the hindquarters of the dog, which had gone completely still. "What's wrong besides me calling you a boy when you're clearly a girl?"

Nothing felt out of place or broken. The pup's whine was consistent. The harder he pulled her toward freedom, the more the dog pressed backward.

The leash was caught on something or the pup was injured. He pulled hard and he still couldn't get the leash free. Blindly he followed the leather to an icy death grip of fingers, causing him to instantly retreat. His jerky reaction scared the dog, causing her to struggle harder in the dark.

"It's okay, sweetheart. Take it easy and I'll get you out of here." Jake kept a firm grip on the collar, snagged the flashlight from his pocket and flipped the switch to take a closer look at the body.

The glassy look of the dead took him back to Afghanistan. He'd experienced that look more than once in his military career. Male or female, it always twisted his gut.

Then it hit him. The smell of death. Faint, most likely because of the cold, but there wafting into his brain and triggering more memories that he wanted to forget. Once experienced, he could never forget.

The call hadn't been a prank. The woman's coat was covered in white. She'd been there all night. He'd flattened the crime scene getting to the dang dog, which wouldn't or couldn't leave her side.

"Hold on there, girl. I'm not going to hurt you. Give me a second here." He couldn't remove the leash from the body. So he'd have to disconnect the dog.

Expensive leash with a word etched into the wet leather. "Dallas? That your name or just a souvenir?" He kept a grip on the Lab with his left hand and unsnapped the leash from the dog harness with his right.

He crooned, attempting to calm the shivering mass of fur. He peeled his jacket off in the cramped space, the sharp broken twigs poking him with every shrug. He draped Dallas and shoved his coat under the dog's legs. He took one last look into the frozen face. There was something about her, or the situation.

Something he couldn't put a name to. Or maybe just a habit he'd started with the first investigation he'd had as a military cop. He didn't want to make the vow. He had a clean slate but couldn't stop the words. "Whoever did this won't get away. And I'll take care of your pup, ma'am. That's a promise."

Unable to move, Dallas didn't struggle much covered in his jacket. Jake pulled her free, shimmying under the fence instead of scaling it, dragging the pup under after. Then he sat on a fallen tree, holding Dallas in his lap. He began to feel the cold as the wind whipped through the secluded jogging path that viewed the spillway overlook and hit his wet clothes.

Dallas made a unique noise halfway between a howl and whine.

"It'll be okay, girl. We'll find you another owner before too long." He stroked the pup's head and she quieted just a bit. Her tags indicated a rabies vaccination and that she'd been chipped, but they'd need Animal Control to access the information.

Jake tried his radio. Nothing. He took his cell from its carrier on his hip. Nothing. He moved up the hill until he had reception and dialed.

"Dallas 911. What's your emergency?"

"This is Detective Jake Craig, badge 5942. I have an expired subject. Bus required at Garland and Winstead parking lot WTR 114 marker."

"An ambulance has been dispatched to your location. Do you need me to connect you to Homicide?" the dispatcher asked.

"Thanks, but we're already here."

"Understood, Detective Craig."

Protocol required him to ask for an ambulance, but he knew it wasn't necessary. The woman frozen to the ground a couple of feet away was dead and had been most of the night. He'd seen the dead before. Many times over and under too many circumstances to remember them all. He didn't want to remember.

Life was easier when he didn't.

The pup tipped her soggy face up at him, and then

rested on his thigh. Jake looked around the crushed crime scene as he dialed his partner's cell. "I don't know about you, Dallas, but it's going to be a helluva long day."

Chapter Two

This murder should have been Jake's. He'd discovered that body—and ruined the crime scene. No one razed him or admonished him for being so stupid.

All of the men thought the dog was great. But it was still his job to control it—not an easy task without a leash. He'd found a silver emergency blanket in the trunk and had fashioned a makeshift rope by slicing the end off.

No words saying he should have left the pup there. Nothing except "four black coffees, Craig," turning him into a glorified errand boy. He had to remember that it was the appropriate place for the rookie team member. He walked to the car with a few laughs and snickers behind his back. His partner hadn't offered the keys. No way he was going to beg, but he could keep the pup warm inside the car while he walked across the street.

A local diner was on the opposite corner. He could handle the errands and understood they came with being the newest team member. He'd dumped enough rookies into the same position himself over the years. He was just ready to move forward, to investigate. He hated being stuck with unimportant things. It gave him too much time to think about the life he'd wanted while in Afghanistan that seemed so far out of his reach.

The tremor he'd forgotten started his hand twitching.

He fisted his fingers and shoved it in his pocket. Out of sight, out of his thoughts. Right along with the dreams he'd had from another time.

"Man alive, it's cold out here." A man waited on the corner to cross Gaston Boulevard, jumping in place to keep warm. "You a cop?"

Jake gave a short nod, not in the mood for curious onlookers. Even those dressed all in black, sturdy shoes and expensive leather gloves. Why was this guy walking anywhere in this weather? *Not everyone's a suspect,* he said, to quiet the suspicions forming in his head.

This wasn't the Middle East, where he couldn't trust a kid crossing the street or even a middle-aged man dressed in black. The light turned red, the walk light blinked on and they both crossed. The man continued to the convenience store next to the diner, probably after cigarettes, since he'd reeked of nicotine.

Jake entered the old-fashioned diner and stuffed his gloves in his pockets. The place was basically empty except for a pretty raven-haired woman in the back booth. As soon as he looked in her direction, she dropped her lips to the edge of the mug and blew, gingerly sipping and not making eye contact.

Nothing suspicious in a young woman wanting to be left alone by a man covered in mud.

A robust man dressed in a bright red-and-black shirt hurried out of the kitchen. He only needed a white beard to look exactly like an off-duty Santa Claus. "Have a seat anywhere," he said, wiping his hands on the bottom of his flannel plaid shirt.

"I just need five coffees to go, Carl." The Santa named Carl looked surprised to hear his name until Jake pointed at his dangling nameplate stuck on his sleeve. "Don't lose that in someone's breakfast."

The woman in the corner laughed, barely, but it was a sweet sound compared to the silent razing he'd been taking for wrecking the murder scene. Sweet, and it brought a smile to his frozen face.

"I was wonderin' how you knew." Carl reached for the cups and coffeepot. "You want cream or sugar?"

"Blacks all round. Thanks."

"Hey, you with the cops at the lake? A guy came in earlier and said you found a body by the dam."

"Detective Jake Craig, Dallas P.D.," Jake acknowledged, trying to dissuade him from asking more questions. It didn't work.

"So was it a woman, like they say? Was she really all in white? Murdered? Froze to death?"

Everyone, including himself, wanted those answers.

"How long have you been at work today?" he asked. If the counter guy wanted to be chatty, might as well point him in the right direction.

"Been here since 'bout midnight, I think. Took a while in this weather with the roads the way they were. I skidded through two different red lights. Glad you weren't around then."

"How about her?" Jake asked about the woman in the corner.

"Bree? She's been here since I came on board."

"That's a long time to nurse a cup of java."

"Nah, happens all the time. And I think that's her fourth or fifth hot chocolate. She nods off every once in a while."

There was a rolling suitcase against the wall next to her. "She homeless?"

"Naw, nothin' like that. Lost her car, broke down a couple of months back, and she walks everywhere. Does jobs for people in Lakewood, picks up an extra shift around here sometimes. Manager don't mind her sitting there when we ain't busy."

"You said she's been here since midnight?" His victim had already been killed by then.

"Yeah, let me get you a carrier for these. I got a new box of 'em in the back," Carl said, putting the last lid on a large cup.

"How much do I owe you?"

"On the house for cops."

After leaving a five, Jake put his wallet away and leaned against the counter, watching the busy intersection. Predawn joggers, walkers with dogs, people driving by and going about their ordinary day. Busy, yet not a single witness. He took the lid off one cup and poured a good amount of sugar in. He'd need the extra calories today.

While he sipped, he watched, honing his skills, making mental notes. Passing the time like he had for so many years.

The woman Carl called Bree shifted in her seat, looking nervous. She'd obviously overheard the conversation with Carl. Most people were more curious for details. When he came across someone who turned away, covered their face and tried to act casual about doing so…it normally meant they were hiding something.

Or was he just being overly suspicious again, wanting to investigate a murder instead of paying his dues by getting coffee?

Stick it out. They'll come around soon enough.

Carl loaded the coffees into the cardboard.

"Thanks, man."

"No problemo. Come back when there's not a murder. Gotta get ready for my breakfast regulars." Carl waved and returned to the kitchen.

"I'll do that." Jake leaned his shoulder against the door,

pushing it open for a fraction of a second. Hit by a blast of frigid air, the coffee carrier tipped toward his filthy coat. He let the door slam, successfully catching the coffees and balancing them against his chest. A tiny giggle from the corner. He looked up and locked eyes with Bree. The woman had a beautiful smile. No matter how brief or even if she was laughing at his near disaster.

She quickly hid her eyes by resting her forehead on her hand. Her reaction made him more than a little curious. He set the container down on the first booth's table and deliberately meandered past the booth that separated them. *Speak.* He stood there, waiting. Expecting…he didn't know what. Anticipation took over his vocal cords, refusing to let them work. He didn't want to ask her why she looked suspicious. He didn't want her to be a suspect or a witness. What he wanted was her phone number.

Naw, he couldn't do that. At least not as a police officer. He hadn't asked for any phone numbers or called any that had been offered to him in the year since his divorce. Dang it. She was a potential witness. He should ask for her information, since she'd been here all night. *Man, that is so weak. Just say something.* His hand had reached inside his coat for his notebook before he realized he needed a pen.

Then her spine straightened, her hands dropped to her lap and she tilted her face up at him. Strikingly magnificent amethyst eyes. He'd never seen that color before.

"Do you need something, Detective?"

"I was…" The pen had been with the notepad earlier. He patted every pocket on his coat. "Can I borrow your pen?"

She didn't turn away, just slid her larger spiral notebook in front of her and handed over the pen from between its pages.

"Thanks."

"If you need one for the crime scene, I'm sure Carl has an extra. That ink's actually pink."

The old saying of a smile lighting up a room popped into his head. He would swear the entire diner had brightened when the corners of her mouth rose, silently amused that he'd be writing with her girlie-colored pen. He shook himself and wrote Carl's name and then *Bree*.

"Ma'am, sorry to disturb you. Carl mentioned you walked here. Did you come through the park?"

"No, not last night. Was someone really murdered?" She visibly relaxed when she answered.

"Unfortunately, yes." Sort of an odd physical reaction to the word *murder. Don't read anything into it.*

"That's so sad."

"Yes, ma'am. Did you see anything unusual? Anyone running from the park or a car speeding away?"

"No. But I slept some after midnight."

"I'd like your name and phone number, just in case we have new information and need to pursue it with you. You never know what detail might help."

"It's really hard to see out of these windows at night, Detective. I really don't think there's a need to put me in a report."

He looked up to see the reflection of a man covered in mud—even on his face. He looked like an extra in a disaster movie. He agreed that from the booth you couldn't really see much outside.

"Not for the report. It's only in case I need to get in touch again. I'd prefer your cell number, if possible. Carl said your name was Bree?" He concentrated on the tip of the pen where it met the paper. Not on the disconcerted twitch that occurred at the corner of her eye when he said he wanted information about her.

"Yes. Bree Bowman. And I don't have a phone, but you

can reach me at 214-964-79— Well, shoot, I always get those last numbers confused." She opened the spiral and removed a yellow flyer. "Here."

"Jerome's Pet Sitters. You work here?" He stuffed the paper in his pocket.

"I fill in when I have time. Jerome takes messages."

"Is Bree short for something?"

"No."

She shifted on the bench, looking as uncomfortable as he felt awkward. He knew cops who used the addresses and numbers of pretty girls. That wasn't his style. He couldn't legitimize pushing for her address. He'd get it if he really needed to get in touch.

"That should be enough for now." He set her pen on the table, watching it roll to the edge of the spiral. "Thanks for your cooperation."

"No problemo," she said, imitating Carl.

"Right. Thanks again." He scooped up the coffees, including his own, and headed for the door.

"Wait. Let me help." Bree's voice came from just behind him. "I can get the door so you don't have a disaster with those cups." She darted around him, pushed the door and kept it open while he passed through.

"Thanks for the help."

"You're very welcome."

Like an idiot he stopped and took another look at her. And like someone who hadn't flirted in a decade—which he hadn't—he said, "You know you have the most beautiful eyes I've ever seen."

She inhaled sharply and pressed her lips together. Maybe embarrassed. Maybe flattered. Maybe like she received that compliment a lot. "Thanks, Detective. But it's really cold out."

"Yeah, sorry. Have a nice day."

"You, too."

Just before the door closed, he heard another sweet giggle.

You're such an idiot.

DAWN CAME AND WENT along with the ambulance and dead woman's body. She'd had no identification, no keys, and to their knowledge, no one had reported her missing. Dallas howled endlessly as her owner was removed by the medical examiner.

The obvious assumption was that the victim had been mugged while walking her dog. Locate where the dog lived and they'd discover the identity of the owner.

Simple.

No one was pursuing it. They'd wait on Animal Control to call with the chip's registered address.

After contaminating the scene, Jake had been told he was lucky to be holding the dog. Coffee run completed, he'd waited in the car. Warmed the dog. Fed the dog his sandwich from home. Watered the dog. Pacified the dog. Everyone else finished up, the crime scene had been released, and he was now letting the dog do his business near a tree.

"Hey, Craig," his partner called to him from across the lot, laughing and slapping the back of another longtime detective. "Make sure you wait around for Animal Control to get that mutt. They're expecting you to be right here, so you should probably walk the dog in circles until they show." He laughed some more and threw the car keys. "I'm catching a ride back to the station."

Jake caught the keys and didn't have a chance to ask his partner what they all found so hilarious before the car pulled away. He stood there holding the pup's makeshift leash, fearing the joke was on him. Yeah, he was darn certain that around the station he'd graduated from the position of rookie to leash holder.

The last patrolman headed to his car, pointing at the ground. "You got a bag to clean that up, man?"

Jake shrugged, then shook his head.

"Seriously, man. You can't leave that on the ground like that."

He shot him a look, hoping the patrolman would back off. "I'll get something from Animal Control."

"You gotta set a good example for the kids over there. Leaving it in a park's against city ordinances. You're a cop now."

"Sure. I got it." And he did…get it. The marines were behind him and he was on his own, alone in a city where he barely knew anyone. He'd wanted that after the divorce. No one around to remind him of the six years of humiliation.

Jake sat in his car and started the engine, thinking of amethyst eyes. A better memory than the wasted time he'd invested with his ex. Should he call Bree Bowman?

And then what? Say what? Do what? Ask her to meet for coffee? Maybe he'd make it a habit to have breakfast at the diner and try to catch her there again. And breakfast to boot. It wasn't too far out of his way. Then he might be able to offer a ride sometime. That was a plan he could live with. Slow. No commitment.

Another twenty minutes went by and more kids on bikes gathered in the parking lot. It looked like they wanted his car out of the way so they could take advantage of the ice and snow.

He moved to the far edge of the lot to give the boys room. Some of the tricks they performed were amazing. It wasn't too much longer before Dallas began whining again, soon howling loud enough to attract attention.

This time she clawed at the window as one of the boys

slowly approached from the curb. Dressed in a ski cap, a huge coat that wasn't zipped, and straddling a bike designed more for tricks than street cruising, the teen waved and gestured to roll down the window.

"Hey, Dallas. You get lost, girl?" the teen crooned to the big pup and stuck his gloved hand through the window to stroke the silky ears. "Whatcha doin' way over here?"

"Do you know this dog or the owner?" Jake asked.

"Sure, this is Dallas. She belongs to Mrs. Richardson. I ride past her house every day. Weird that she ran away. She sticks pretty close to home even when she gets loose." The teen continued to pet the pup through the open window. "You a cop? One of the other guys said a drunk froze to death. He got a look at the body bag."

"Would you happen to know her address?"

"It's five or six houses up on Loving Street. The one on the hill. I can take her back if you want. She's run next to my bike before."

"Thanks, but I better hang on to her. What does the house look like?"

He shrugged. "We can show you. Nothing to do around here anymore. It's getting too wet."

"Thanks. There's no rush. Make sure to use the crosswalks."

"It's the second street, mister." The teen turned and tapped the hood before peddling off through the snow. "Try to keep up."

Jake pushed the button to roll up the window and put the car in gear. Dallas turned three circles on the passenger seat before settling. She dropped her head in the crook of Jake's elbow and looked up with dark brown sad eyes.

"It'll be okay, sweetheart." He scratched the pup's snout and then picked up the car radio. "You'll be okay. Somebody with a great yard will snatch you up quick."

One by one the boys followed each other, skidding through the parking lot, enjoying the snow and slush. Sometimes, being a kid had its advantages. No worries and no past.

"Dispatch, Craig to Loving and Winstead. Cancel the Animal Control pickup at White Rock Lake. I'll call back if needed later." He turned on the second street, following the kid he'd spoken with while the others continued straight.

"Detective Craig, no record of a request for Animal Control. Your location is noted."

The other detectives were probably having a big laugh at breakfast with this joke. He'd been left holding a dog leash, waiting for the past two hours on Animal Control when they'd never been notified. Some joke.

But he'd take the hazing. This time it might just work in his favor. When he'd spoken his opinion that the dog had a connection to the murder victim, his partner had put him in charge of the animal.

He'd either return Dallas to her owner without anyone the wiser or call in the identity of the dead woman. Maybe he'd get the last laugh after all.

Chapter Three

Two weeks in one bed. Sabrina could barely believe how much she looked forward to having the same pillow under her head for that long. Living out of a suitcase, shuffling from house to house or a couple of nights in a hotel room had gotten old after the fourth or fifth time. Six months later and she wasn't any closer to discovering Griffin's connection to whoever had ordered her death or who they'd referred to as the "higher-ups."

She was ready to give up her search and her nomad existence. Griffin had accused her of not having a life. Well, he'd been wrong. Her life had been full of people and pets and things to care about. It was living like this that wasn't really living. If that even made sense. A solitary life void of friends and fun. Shoot, she didn't even have a car.

And to top it off, the first inkling of an attraction she'd had was for a cop. A detective she'd nearly given her cell number to. Yes, she'd lied to the detective about owning a cell. What if he'd actually called? What a stupid move that would have been. But he'd seemed so…so shy.

She lifted the suitcase out of the slush as she crossed the last street.

Walking through a little snow wasn't hard for a girl born and raised in the Texas Panhandle. No, sir, a little snow and ice didn't slow her down at all. She walked the four blocks from the coffee shop to her next pet-sitting job, pulling her handy-dandy suitcase. Barely any cars passed by. She'd taken the long way around to avoid the park just in case the detective was still nearby. From her view at the diner, it had appeared empty with the exception of one car and the local kids on their bikes.

Dallas with a layer of snow was a lot different than Amarillo in the same condition. Back home on a Saturday morning all the kids would have been on that hilltop, sliding until their fingers were frozen from grabbing the edge of their plastic or even cardboard sled. She couldn't let herself think of home.

Thinking of the people she'd hurt by running away wouldn't help her get home any sooner. At first, she hadn't contacted her parents because she hadn't wanted anyone in danger from the men working with Griffin. She soon realized being dead made getting around much easier. Law enforcement wasn't searching for her.

Even if the police weren't looking, it didn't mean she could see the handsome detective. That would be thumbing her nose at the good fortune she'd had for the past six months. Sooner or later her luck would run out.

Each day she hoped her family would forgive her when she finally proved her innocence and could go home again. There were three more names to check out and then she'd have to turn herself in to the police. Or use the stolen money to hire a detective to clear her name.

She couldn't do that. The money was evidence. If she'd used it, she could have gone anywhere, hired that dang detective months ago, slept in a nice hotel instead of those shelters the first week. Other than the three hundred dollars she'd been forced to use, over ninety thousand dollars—in very large bills—was now hidden in the liner of her toiletry bag. She'd only grabbed one bundle and hidden the rest with her uncle, who'd helped her leave Amarillo.

Sabrina peeled off her gloves and found her keys in her jacket pocket. She pushed the handle of the suitcase down. The huge monster was wearing out along the bottom faster than the first one she'd bought secondhand. Obtaining another needed to be added to her list of things to get done soon.

Think about that in two weeks. Maybe living out of a suitcase won't be necessary then.

Stomping her wet tennis shoes on the welcome mat, she wished again she had her favorite snow boots. She tried to get as much snow off them as possible before entering Brenda Ellen's immaculate domain and just pulled them off instead, along with her wet socks. She turned her key in the kitchen door, dropping the set into her pocket.

Backing inside, she lifted her case over the threshold, bracing for Dallas's welcome. The big, rambunctious pup could knock her down when she caught her off guard.

No Dallas.

She whistled while shrugging out of her coat and dropping it along with her shoes on top of the suitcase. She clapped. Still no sound of nails clicking on the hardwood floors.

"Dallas," she called. "Mrs. Richardson? Brenda Ellen?"

Had her trip been delayed again because of the snow? Dirty dishes sat on the counter and stove. Weird, because Brenda Ellen Richardson practically ate over the sink when she bothered to eat at home. The loaf of bread was open. Grease in a frying pan where eggs had been cooked. Blood near a block of cheese on the counter.

"Oh, God."

Was that Brenda Ellen's blood? Or had someone else made themselves at home?

Brenda Ellen didn't eat eggs and never fried anything. Had they found her? *No! No! No!* Don't panic. Maybe Brenda Ellen had forgotten to text her that the flight had been delayed. Maybe she'd had company overnight. *That* potential scene was embarrassing but held much less panic.

But where was Dallas? Even if she was locked out of Brenda Ellen's bedroom, she'd be greeting any visitor at the door.

Something was wrong. Brenda Ellen was a business-woman and wouldn't have forgotten to cancel her dog sitter. Should she leave? *Yes, turn and run this minute!* Grabbing the suitcase and running down the sidewalk was the safest thing to do.

And then what? She could go…where?

If someone was here, they'd heard her come inside, heard her whistle for Dallas. They'd follow her down the street. What if they were waiting for her to search the house? What if Brenda Ellen was tied up or…or…worse?

I'm so tired of being afraid, she said to herself.

It was time to stop being afraid and confront the fear. Take action. Do something proactive and not just run. Dial 911 and then leave.

Her cell was packed. Fortunately, or it would have been in plain sight for Detective Jake Craig. *Then get to the landline in the living room, and get help for Brenda Ellen, then leave.* That was a plan. She'd taken self-defense classes. She could get to the phone on Brenda Ellen's desk.

As quietly as possible, she rolled open the drawer that contained the meat mallet. The knives were tempting, but much bigger than the scalpel she'd stabbed Griffin with.

Attempting to get to Brenda Ellen's phone was risky. But she couldn't leave without trying, without knowing if her employer needed help. If Brenda Ellen was in trouble, it was Sabrina's fault and she had to do whatever she could.

Mallet in hand, she knelt at the doorway, trying to see if anyone waited in the living area. Surely, if anyone were there, they would have already come to see who had whistled and clapped. There wasn't anything to be frightened of. Unfortunately, she couldn't stop shaking or thinking about the different possibilities. Overreacting had become the new normal for her.

"There's nothing there." Sabrina stood and shook the tension from her arms but kept the mallet in her hands.

She rounded the corner, prepared to whack any intruder or at least throw the mallet at their head. Nothing. The pillows were out of place, the cushions were crooked and the glass top on the coffee table was shattered.

It might look like an accident had happened, but she knew Brenda Ellen. The woman had given her a five-minute lecture when she hadn't vacuumed one morning.

She froze. Had that been wood creaking? Barely a sound from the carpeted stairs, but she recognized it. Being in the house alone with Dallas, she'd heard it many nights as the pup had gone downstairs to bark and howl. She swallowed hard, the simple silent sound reverberating in her head like a shout. She held her breath.

Was it the man from the clinic? The one who looked like he enjoyed killing? His horrible smile haunted her nightmares where she was endlessly being chased.

Whoever was behind her on the stairs knew she was in the house. She couldn't make it across the room to the phone. She couldn't unbolt the front door without her keys, which were in the pocket of her coat. Out the kitchen door was her only choice.

So she ran. She hated turning her back, afraid the crazy-smile guy would shoot her between the shoulders. Unlike her dreams, where she ran all night, just out of his reach. He heard her. She could hear his heavy, fast-paced steps.

The lamp from the sofa table toppled to the floor behind her as she skidded around the corner of the kitchen.

Don't look. Don't look. Don't look.

She slid to a stop, yanked the door open as far as her suitcase allowed and jumped the two steps to the driveway.

"Hi, Bree, looking for Dallas?"

It took a couple of seconds to shove her heart from her throat to her chest again. It was just a neighborhood kid she'd met plenty of times while walking the dogs. "Get out of here, Joey."

"It's okay. This cop found her at the lake. I guess she got out after Mrs. Richardson left."

"Cop? Where?" She grabbed his bike handles and pulled. "Come on, Joey. I said to get going."

"What's wrong?" he asked, dragging his feet through the drifting snow.

The door swung open. She caught a glimpse of a barrel, a man in a mask. "Get down!"

Sabrina jerked the handle bars sideways, knocking Joey to the ground and jumping on top of him. A beige blur pulled her sweater and shoved her facedown into the snow next to the street.

"Hold it," a deep voice boomed from above her.

"He's…he's in the house with a gun," she explained, spitting the snow from her mouth.

"You okay, kid?" the voice asked. Nothing like the voice from the clinic. The tones floating to her ears were deep and rich with a natural Texas twang she recognized.

Jake Craig.

She watched Joey's head bob up and down and then an excited gleam dart into his eyes at the thought of danger. *Give it up. It ain't anything like you think it might be, kid.*

"Stay here," the voice commanded as he ran toward the door.

They'd do no such thing.

She was getting Joey as far away from the house as possible. "Get behind that car," she told Joey, who seemed mesmerized.

"But he said—"

"I don't care. Get up and move."

Faster than she thought possible, they were sitting with their backs against the tires. She expected gunfire to explode around them at any moment. The more seconds that ticked by, the easier she breathed, and the more she realized she needed to sneak away before the cop returned.

Her feet were stinging from the cold. Could she get somewhere safe without any shoes?

Scratching against glass. She heard a familiar bark and whine. *Dallas*.

The pup was in good hands. The cop would take care of everything. She could leave without him ever really seeing her face. She shivered from the cold, wiping melting snow from her skin. She could get another used coat when she picked up a new suitcase.

Oh, no! The money!

Whether it was her exasperated cry of utter disappointment or her slow recovery from having been scared to death, Joey responded with an awkward pat on her shoulder.

"Was there really someone inside with a gun?" the teen asked, unable to hide the excitement in his voice. "Was she, like, being robbed or something?"

He started to stand and she tugged him back to her side.

"How did Dallas end up with a policeman? What's going on?"

"See, we was, like, going down to do some stunts in the empty lot and instead there was a lot of cop cars. They hauled somebody off in, like, a real body bag and everything. Then we notice this guy and he had Dallas. So I went over and asked him why."

During the explanation, her heart ventured into another part of her body again. "Do you know who died?"

Dallas barked, pawing at the door.

"You're Mrs. Richardson?" the detective asked, coming around the end of his car. "Is this your dog?"

"Nope, this is Bree. She's the dog sitter," Joey answered.

Jake had a strange look on his face. He listened intently the entire time and never took his eyes off her. Sabrina knew he was tall. He'd towered over her at the diner, but from a sitting position on the ground, he was frighteningly tall. It didn't help that his wary approach seemed ominous. She knew he was legit and not a part of the higher-ups, but she couldn't stop shaking.

"Can I go now?" Joey asked, touching her hand.

She hadn't known she still held the teen's arm. She released him and the cop came closer. He didn't slide around on the quickly defrosting ice. But his clothes looked like he'd already taken a couple of bad spills. She'd seen them in detail at the diner.

"Thanks for the directions, kid."

"I gotta go tell everybody what happened," Joey said. He was down the hill and nearly around the corner by the time she turned to face Jake.

Jake? Detective Craig! The same detective who does not need your phone number, she realized. *Oh, my gosh.* She was even rambling nervously in her thoughts.

"Hold on a minute, sweetheart."

"What?"

He reached past her and stuck his arm inside the car, then swung the door open and Dallas leaped out. The pup joined her, crowding her face with a cold nose. She automatically began running her fingers across the pup's sides. While her chin was being licked, Bree shifted her gaze from the ground, connecting with the detective's curious observation.

The images of a gun, body bags, jail... They all circled her head, making it swim. *Brenda Ellen would have been walking Dallas last night.* She felt desperately ill and dropped her face into the black fur.

"You didn't catch him?" she asked.

"I didn't find anyone, no."

"Is she...? Is that why you were bringing Dallas home?" *Oh, my gosh, she's dead.* Sabrina could tell she was right by the detective's sympathetic sigh and awkwardness.

"I need to ask you a few questions, Miss Bowman." He extended his hand to help her stand.

Sabrina had no choice. Because of her, Brenda Ellen had died. Perhaps she should be arrested and leave the investigating to professionals. She placed her cold fingers within his warm grip and stood. She didn't want to go to jail. "I'm Bree."

"Yeah, I remember."

He kept hold of her hand, steadying her. Gone was the shyness, the awkward bit of flirtation from the diner. They stood there for several seconds until Dallas whimpered and pawed at her legs.

"Maybe we should go inside?" he asked.

"Can we? After that guy was there? I mean, don't you need fingerprints or something? He killed Brenda Ellen."

"Did you actually see someone?" He shoved into her hand some silver material that he'd used for a leash, then tugged her to the sidewalk, protectively pushing her a couple of feet behind a giant sycamore. She winced as the snow covered her feet.

"He pointed a gun at Joey out the door. The kitchen's a wreck and you said someone killed her."

"I didn't say anything."

"Didn't you?"

"No."

"But you found a body and Dallas was at the lake. There's eggs and grease and a mess." She wasn't making sense and, from his curious expression, could tell he was confused.

"Did you actually see someone in the house?"

"Yes. He chased me outside and was going to shoot us, but then you got here."

"What makes you think that? What did he look like?"

"I don't know. He had a mask and a gun. I saw the gun." Her hands shook. She hadn't been this frightened since stabbing Griffin with a scalpel. "She never, ever eats fried food."

"Ma'am, I'm having a hard time following. You aren't making much sense. I didn't find anyone inside, but I can check it out if you want to wait in the car."

"HE KILLED HER, didn't he?"

Bree Bowman was losing it and sort of melted onto the sidewalk along with the snow from the night before. He didn't believe she'd actually fainted but it was close. Jake did the only thing he knew how to do...

He grabbed the leash and lifted Bree. She was a tiny thing, fitting easily into his arms. She was crying hard, and was half-frozen from being outside without a coat or shoes. Her tiny feet were a bluish color, waving in the air. His only option was the house. Crime scene or not.

The door banged half open again. He took a second to look this time at what it hit. He recognized the suitcase from the diner—so she was a house sitter, not only a dog walker. The bottom of the case was still wet, so she hadn't been there long. She clung to the dog leash and Dallas pulled them a couple of steps forward. Jake whacked his hip on a drawer.

"I'm so sorry. I needed the meat mallet in case someone attacked."

"Drop the leash, Bree."

"I can't." She locked her arms around his neck, pulling herself closer. "She'll run through the house, maybe destroy evidence. She's certain to get into things and someone was here. They chased me."

"I've got it. You can let go." She searched his eyes and then let go as instructed.

When he set her on her feet, he kept an arm around her waist to steady her. Dallas continued to tug and beg to be free.

"What makes you think your boss didn't just have an overnight guest who didn't clean up after himself and maybe thought *you* were the intruder?"

"Brenda Ellen was scheduled to leave for Seattle yesterday. Her flight was canceled and she was rescheduled for eleven o'clock this morning," Bree whispered. "She wouldn't have left anything out of place. She never does."

Jake searched the kitchen. It was immaculate compared to his apartment. "Look, even if someone was here earlier, they're gone now."

"How do you know they aren't hiding? Where'd they go? All the doors are still closed. What if someone was with the man with the gun?"

"I checked out the perimeter and backyard." He needed to follow procedure and begin from the beginning. But instead, he broke protocol and placed his hands on Bree's shoulders, trying to reassure her it would be okay.

Great, he hadn't even called the location into his partner or captain yet. If someone had been there, they were long gone. He had little hope of a BOLO. Bree inhaled and opened her mouth to speak again. He covered her parted lips with a finger. Her warm breath escaped, but she didn't utter a sound.

"I'm going to call for backup. You're going to stay here with Dallas. Try to keep her quiet. Nod if you understand?"

She barely moved. He wanted to dab her wet lashes and give her a long hug. Why? Maybe it was the sympathy he felt for the dog spilling over to this petite, caring woman. Or the way she'd giggled at him in the diner. He didn't know and squashed the urge.

"One thing first. What did Brenda Ellen Richardson look like?"

"Dark brown hair, about my length, slender, average height."

"What color were her eyes?"

"Were? She's…then she *is* who you found at the lake. They're brown."

She described his murder victim. With his luck, he'd be destroying more evidence by searching the house, but he needed to secure it. He pulled his cell from its belt holster. "Wait here."

Jake called for backup and moved methodically through the rest of the house. Once he was in the front room, he saw a picture of his murder victim, laughing with an older couple. Most likely her parents. And then another of her with a golden retriever. He called his partner, giving him the name and address, and hung up before the old goat could gripe at him for being inside the house.

The furniture was nice, no dust on the shelves, a variety of books in the hallway case. From his point of view, barely anything was out of place. Breakfast dishes, a drop of blood from slicing cheese and a cracked coffee table that could have happened when the dog ran through the house. It didn't look like there'd been an intruder.

But he entered each room as if an AK-47 was on the opposite side of the door. He couldn't help it. Old habits were hard to break. His last partner had laughed a couple of times, but it had quickly become a routine for them. Better safe than sorry.

A dress was lying on the bedspread—could have been worn Friday or laid out for today, he couldn't tell. Two nice suitcases sat in the corner by the master bath, giving credence to Bree's story.

The house was clear. His backup should be here in a few minutes. Time to get some information from his witness and get himself back on this case. He headed downstairs and Dallas greeted him halfway up. "So you got loose. Overanxious?"

He hooked his hand in the leash and spent a couple of minutes coaxing the pup to go with him.

"I need to ask you a couple of questions now." He entered the kitchen, but his witness was no longer there. Gone, along with the coat and suitcase.

He'd fallen for her act, hook, line and sinker.

Chapter Four

"Dark hair, amethyst eyes, about five-three or -four. Looks a lot like the victim from the back. Nothing like her up close. Probably about twenty-five." If Jake went into detail about the heart shape of her face, the petite bone structure or how he'd noticed the way her nose curved at the tip and had five distinct freckles, his partner would think him nuts. Or might believe Jake had let her go deliberately.

As it was, the razing hadn't ceased since Detective Elton Owens had shown up to continue the investigation. More precisely, the murder investigation that didn't involve Jake. Owens stood there, checking his notes, treating Jake like a suspect. Or worse, like a naive rookie.

"You say you saw her at the diner this morning? And you didn't think to mention this when you returned with coffee?"

"Come on, Owens. There was no way to know she was the victim's house sitter. You'd still be waiting on Missing Persons or the chip information about the dog if I hadn't followed the kids here." And Animal Control, if it hadn't been for the kids. He knew he was acting defensively and was just tired enough not to care.

Owens ignored him and asked the crime scene investigator some questions.

Jake knew he'd been a good police officer over the past

year. He'd accepted being the low man on the totem pole in Homicide, accepting the grunt work, not caring how many hours he worked without pay. He didn't have a life outside of the job and didn't want one. Working over Christmas had kept him from a face-to-face meeting with his parents, siblings and other relatives.

Being around his family made him uncomfortable. Being grilled by his partner was almost as bad.

His family had never asked if the accusations his ex-wife had made were true, but they'd also never said the words were lies. Maybe they interpreted his embarrassment for being blind to his wife's indiscretions, somehow making him the guilty party. After a while, it just didn't matter. It was easier to let sleeping dogs lie and avoid confrontations about his disastrous marriage. He was moving past his first wife and the war.

Thing about it—he *was* past his ex. And that was the hardest part for his parents to understand. Sad, but whatever had been there in the beginning of his marriage had slipped away after spending months and thousands of miles apart over the past six years.

When the position opened in Dallas—three hours from his hometown in east Texas—he jumped at it. He needed a new start and it was easier that way. A year later and he was working in Homicide. Exactly where he wanted to be.

Now his partner assumed he'd made mistakes instead of decisions. He'd like someone—anyone—to trust his judgment. No one really had since he'd left the corps. Well, he couldn't actually blame them. He'd let the witness escape. Bree had turned on the waterworks and he'd been suckered in, big-time.

Bamboozled. That's right, Craig, teased the devil sitting on his shoulder.

Owens removed the picture from the frame. "Definitely

our victim. Looks like we need to find her parents to no-
tify. The dog sitter, this Bree woman, you say she seemed
more frightened that someone was in the house than that
Mrs. Richardson had been murdered."

"I didn't say that, Owens. She was visibly upset about
both instances." *I think.*

"When you get back to the station, you can spend the
day looking through mug shots. We'll be taking a hard look
at Richardson's finances, see if we can find payment to
this mysterious dog sitter. Right now, she's our only lead."
He closed the notebook, returning it to his jacket pocket.
"You sure she was a dog sitter?"

"Joey knew her and seemed to trust her."

"No last name on the kid or any of the other kids?" he
asked, but barely paused. "I'll get a sketch artist to the
diner and an officer moving house to house. Shouldn't be
too hard to locate this chick. Oh, and the captain wants to
see you when you return."

"I figured."

Owens left the house, laughing as he stood on the porch
talking to the first responding officer—as luck would have
it—the same guy who had told him to set a good example
for the kids at the park.

"It'll get easier, you know," Shirley, the crime scene
analyst, interrupted his self-deprecation.

He stopped himself from asking what she referred to
by compressing his lips together. He knew the answer, just
didn't want to have the conversation.

"The ribbing goes away. This is how they treat all the
new guys."

"Find anything?" He'd rather hear about the case—even
if he wasn't officially a part of the investigation.

"It will all be in my report. I'd rather not take wild
guesses."

"Hey, this is Jake Craig, the detective who's not officially on the case. Can't you give me the unofficial version? It won't go any further. Promise." He flashed her a smile, hoping it did the trick. Blatant flirting never hurt.

"Okay. It looks like she was killed at the park. Only a drop of blood in the kitchen and no real struggle other than in the living room."

"Any fingerprints? The dog sitter said the victim kept things clean and lived alone."

"The table does appear to have been shattered today. Very few of the pieces were ground deeply into the carpet. The prints left around the house are fresh and easy to find. We'll rule out the victim's easily enough."

"So it was wiped clean?"

"I don't think so. I agree with the missing dog sitter. I believe the victim did like things clean and took care of it almost daily." His confusion must have appeared on his face since Shirley continued. "Look around you. The owner of this house had a black dog and white carpet. Either the dog didn't live inside, or someone was meticulous about cleaning."

"Got it. What about the footprints in the backyard?" he asked as the analyst gathered her gear. "Anything there?"

Jake stuck his hands in his pockets. He caught a glimpse of his tattered appearance in the mirror and pushed his shoulders back, standing tall. His mother had taught him he looked defeated when he slouched. He wouldn't let this situation defeat him.

The marines corrected the high school self-consciousness of being six inches taller than everyone else around him. But his first week out of uniform, faced with a divorce, living with his parents and not having a future had his mother badgering him to stand up straight on more than one occasion.

"With the layer of snow and ice, it's impossible to gather

anything. Let's just say the little bit of evidence I've collected won't be the strongest lead for solving this homicide." She slipped into her coat.

"Did you catch what the medical examiner surmised was the cause of death?" Definitely strangulation in his opinion. He'd seen the same bloodred eyes on a marine killed by a local militant.

"This isn't official, mind you, but the M.E. noted the subconjunctival hemorrhages before they moved the body." With the last of her winter wear in place, she lifted her cases and flashed him a smile. "In layman terms, she was strangled."

He followed her to the front door and held the outer one open, lowering his voice. "Sounds premeditated if they made it look like it happened while walking her dog and then came back here to cook themselves breakfast."

"Came back is right. They estimated her TOD sometime between eight and eleven last night."

Premeditated and yet the death wasn't violent like a lovers' quarrel. The guy had probably strangled her while she was walking the dog.

Heartless? Had they left the pup to freeze or not killed the dog because they liked animals? Premeditation bugged him. It didn't fit. The murderer seemed to be waiting around for something—or somebody—*after* the murder. Had the dog sitter taken them by surprise or had they been lying in wait?

Exactly who had she been running from when he drove up and why had she run when he was upstairs?

"Shirley?" He caught up with her on the front walk. "I need a favor." Jake handed her his business card. "Can you send the results from the fingerprint search to me? Specifically the one you lifted from the kitchen drawer. That's my cell."

"Sure, but I thought Owens said—"

"Yeah, the favor is you're not going to tell him I know."

"Oh, that won't be a problem. So you think we'll find a match." Shirley stashed his card in her pocket.

"She was too scared for her knees to work. And there is the fact that she ran without putting on her shoes." As indicated by two sets of bare footprints that led into the street.

"It would seem so." Shirley smiled and picked up her case. "I meant to ask, what happened to the dog from this morning?"

"Animal Control showed up this time." It helped when they were actually called—which he'd done personally. "A kid saw Dallas with me at the park and led me here."

"That was lucky, then. I hope someone claims her. Big, black dogs don't get adopted so easily, especially ones with a blind eye. See ya." She waved and got into her car.

Jake sat in his car. "Blind eye? I couldn't tell she was half-blind. Dallas is a good pup. Somebody will adopt her."

The dog deserved someone with a huge yard. Or someone close to a park where she could be trained to catch flying disks or retrieve tennis balls. From the little he'd seen of her interaction with Bree, Dallas had a huge heart. And the loyalty she'd displayed staying with her owner and fighting not to leave her side after she'd been freed, sort of reminded him of his marine brothers.

Would a pup like that get adopted? Or was it amazing she'd been adopted the first time. He'd seen genuine relief on his mystery woman's face when he'd walked up with Dallas. Call it a hunch or good detective work, but he'd bet his next paycheck that Bree wouldn't let Dallas stay overnight in the city pound.

Owens and the rest of the responders were out front, walking toward their vehicles. If he was right about the dog sitter showing up to rescue Dallas, he'd obtain the answers to many of his questions. Official case or not, it wouldn't stop him from finding the murderer.

He'd stared into Brenda Ellen Richardson's death gaze. He was connected to her. He'd also held a half-frozen dog walker in his arms and hoped somehow he was wrong about why she'd been so dang frightened. And especially wrong about why she'd run away.

After a series of calls, Jake finally got the information he needed and the pound location. He circled through a hamburger joint and dealt with his stomach's insistence to be fed. Two burgers and twenty minutes later, he parked in the far corner of the parking lot at the Dallas Animal Services and waited.

Late on a Saturday afternoon, there weren't too many people around. Most of the visitors had a kid or two with them. When a woman driving a really nice ride pulled to a stop, Jake's attention perked up.

Sure enough, less than fifteen minutes later, she had Dallas on a leash and was loading her into the backseat. Jake didn't have to tail the woman closely. They were following the path they'd both taken to get there…straight back to White Rock Lake.

And straight back to Bree.

Chapter Five

"Who's that hunky man? Nice car, but he looks like he wallowed in the snow a couple of times today." Julie brazenly ogled the detective while handing Dallas's leash to Sabrina.

The detective from Brenda Ellen's house? Here? She couldn't turn to look. Maybe he hadn't seen her.

Strong hands landed on her shoulders and long fingers locked her in place inches from his chest. "There you are, Bree. Sorry, I'm a little early."

Oh, shoot. What should she do?

Sabrina hid her surprise as the detective came to her side, tugged her hand from her pocket and locked his fingers with hers. His fingers were warm and his grip secure. His nearness turned her inner thermostat up several degrees. At least he hadn't shoved her face into the picnic table and slapped cuffs on her.

Detective Craig was being gracious and sparing her the embarrassment of an arrest in front of a friend and employer. Julie was just an employer. The only one home who could go pick up Dallas from the pound. And only after Bree had agreed to look after her dogs without charge once.

"Oh, hi, I'm Julie Butler," she bubbled. "No wonder you didn't mind the cold, Bree. Having such a nice guy to warm you back up."

"Sorry to rush you two, but we should probably get

going," he said. "Got to run by my place for some different duds."

Sabrina caught a glimpse of his free hand pointing at his mud-stained pants.

"You two are going out. That's good. Bree shouldn't be alone tonight. Did she tell you Brenda Ellen was murdered?"

"Yes, I was the first person she spoke to about it." He patted her hand. "You're like ice, Bree. We need to get you in front of the car heater."

She'd let him know just how inappropriate he was behaving. Later. Right now, she was grateful not to say another word.

"I should get her home." He kept her hand firmly sealed in his, anchoring her in place.

"Terrible about Brenda Ellen. I'll never feel safe out here again. But Bree, dear, you promised to give me all the details if I picked up Dallas for you." Julie emphasized her fright by dropping her hand across her rather large breasts.

"Another time," the detective said.

"We'll see you in two weeks to sit with the dogs. We're gone four nights and you can bring Dallas with you to the house. If you need to, that is."

"Thanks for picking her up, Julie."

"Ta-ta for now."

Another of her house-sitting jobs walked away. Sabrina acknowledged it would probably be the last time she saw her. If she got away from the police, she'd have to leave all the dogs she worked with.

"Should I thank you, Detective? Or demand a lawyer? Very clever of you to track me down through Dallas. How did you know I wouldn't leave her in the pound?"

"I have to admit I was stuck the first couple of hours, thinking more about what would make you run from the police. But the forensics analyst said black dogs were less likely to be adopted. Then she mentioned the pup was blind in one eye—totally missed that. She seems normal enough."

"She is," she said, defending the puppy.

"I didn't think you'd risk an adoption. Care to answer a couple of questions before we call a lawyer?"

"Well, as you can see, I'm extremely busy right now." She pointed to Dallas, who was doing her best to get off the cold ground. Her scrambling included jumping and slapping her large front paws against Bree's chest.

"Busy leaving?" He pointed to the suitcase just inside a row of bushes.

"Oh, I haven't been home yet. I needed to wait close by for Julie."

"And is home close, since you seem to be walking everywhere? Wait, you ran away five hours ago and haven't made it home and couldn't wait it out at the diner. They put an officer on the place. So you really are cold. I'll be glad to give you a lift so we can chat where it's warm or we could just head directly to see my captain."

"I'm sure we can clear this up right here." She sat at the picnic table, where she'd been waiting since Julie texted.

"I need to see your ID." He extended a hand from the end of the table.

She felt like Jack facing the giant in the fairy tale. "I, um, I lost it about three weeks ago."

"No driver's license? Convenient. Can you remember the number? Or let's try a simple question. One not too taxing on your elusive memory. What's your real name?" He crossed his arms, acting as if he didn't expect a real answer. "Think you can manage that?"

She had barely met him this morning, but she could already tell that the slight curve of the left side of his mouth meant trouble.

"I beg your pardon?"

"Beg all you want, but until I find out who you are—" he paused, digging into his back pocket and then swinging a pair of handcuffs on the tips of two fingers "—you're under arrest."

"For what?" Of course she knew, suspicion of murder, fleeing a crime scene, impeding an investigation. They'd pile on the charges and detain her. Then they'd find out that everyone she cared about in Amarillo thought she was dead. As soon as the police discovered she wasn't, she'd be charged with the murder of whoever was in the clinic fire. And she shouldn't forget about the embezzling and fraud charges that would be sure to follow.

Yes, she knew the answer to her own question…even if this cute detective didn't.

"Fleeing the scene will get us started. I'm certain you're wanted for something, since you're pretty good at avoiding your real name." He gestured for her to hold out her hands to be cuffed. "You know we're going to find out from the prints. Right?"

She held both her hands in front of her, hoping they'd be loosely snapped over her thick gloves. No such luck. He pulled the black fur down, his thumb caressing her pulse.

Did he feel her heart racing?

He took the leash, put a hand on her head and guided her into the backseat of his car. He pulled the shoulder strap and buckled her inside, then gave Dallas a kiss-kiss sound and a gentle tug on her leash. The big, smiling Lab jumped across her, did a couple of turns and settled her head in Bree's lap.

"I hate to ask, but could you get my suitcase? It's on the other side of the bushes."

"Yeah, I saw it."

The door shut, the locks clicked and she was alone while the detective retrieved her stuff. As soon as his back was turned, she tried the door.

Childproof locks. She was stuck. Caught. Going to jail. She stroked Dallas's soft fur, loving the comforting companionship. Somehow she just didn't feel alone when the dog was around.

"Well, girl, I'm not certain what's going to happen now. It breaks my heart to send you back to the pound."

Dallas answered with a sweet sound just like she understood and was commiserating. Brenda Ellen had adopted Dallas four months ago and, honestly, probably never should have. The businesswoman traveled almost twice a month and was gone at least a week for each trip. "I've spent more time with you than she did. Isn't that right, sweetheart?"

Sabrina dropped her cheek to the top of Dallas's head. She was such a loving dog. The trunk opened and closed. It was time to explain everything to Detective Jake Craig. He was her last hope.

"Any chance you're as hungry as I am?" she asked when he was inside the car and had adjusted the rearview mirror to see her.

"I grabbed a burger across the street from the pound while following your friend."

"Oh."

That new look crossing his face lifted one side of his tightly closed mouth, but it clearly indicated pity. She'd learned to recognize it very quickly, hating each time she'd received it over the past six months. But today, right this very minute, it seemed like a sign that her story may not fall on deaf ears.

"I've got some cold fries." He held them out, his long arm extending over Dallas's head.

"Thanks." She shifted her position and held her hands out to take the carton. "Maybe this will keep my stomach from grumbling."

"You should be glad I've got you in custody."

"You think I should be glad to be on my way to jail?" She hated the prospect of being framed and having no one on her side trying to discover the truth.

"Who said anything about jail? Right now I just want some questions answered."

When her family was notified she was alive, they'd be bombarded with questions and accusations, too. They'd only be happy for a moment, learning to hate her very quickly. They'd believe if she could lie about her death, she could lie about a murder.

They'd match her prints since they were on file with the state because of her business. He'd be questioning her right up until they discovered she was a dead woman. But she wasn't—Brenda Ellen was. How had things gotten so out of control?

"Couldn't I just answer your questions here?" she asked, hoping.

She gulped. The dry, cold fry didn't want to go down.

"I don't think that's a good idea." He draped his arm across the seat and stared. Stared straight into her eyes without blinking, without darting those hypnotic deep brown spheres anywhere else. "See, I know your secret, Bree."

This man did something to her. Stirred something she hadn't ever experienced before and couldn't name. Roughly along the lines of instant trust, because he was gaining intimate knowledge without any words. If he searched her inside as deeply as his stare indicated he would, what would he find? An innocent woman had died because of her, didn't that make her guilty now?

She swallowed hard, needing to break the silent interrogation he'd begun. "So you know I love working as a dog walker and moonlight as a serial killer?"

"You're a funny gal." He turned the key and faced her again after putting the car in Reverse. "I know that Brenda Ellen Richardson wasn't the intended victim. You were."

Chapter Six

The silence in the backseat surprised him. Jake expected lots of tears from those magnificent amethyst eyes. Along with a healthy dose of denial and persuasive words attempting to get him to release her.

Dallas whined and nudged the fry container from Bree's lap so she could drop her head there. A moment later Bree buried her face in the pup's fur and he heard a few long intakes of breath as she slowed the tears to a stop.

"I probably shouldn't have sprung it on you like that," he admitted, but gauging her reaction had seemed important. Not so much now.

She wiped both her eyes with the edge of her coat sleeve. "Oh, my gosh, stop being so nice to me and let's just get this done. Haul me to jail so I can tell them everything."

Another unusual reaction.

"Why don't we just start with your real name?"

"It's Bree."

"Do you know who's after you?"

"Can't we just go to the police station, Detective? I don't think the man who killed Brenda Ellen is going to give up as easily as the rest of the police."

"You're with me now and only ten minutes away from a holding cell. I think you're safe enough." Jake put the car into gear and pulled away from the curb. "I've got a hunch you're running from someone. I can help, Bree."

"I know you think you can, Detective. But I seriously doubt you will. I don't think anyone will believe me."

Something twisted in Jake's gut. How many times had he said those words to himself? Why bother explaining what had happened when no one was going to believe him. He'd been convicted without a trial by his family, but he hadn't put up a defense, either.

"Why don't you try me?"

Bree's eyes came to life when they met his in the mirror. He could see the indecision and decided to listen. He turned off the main road and pulled into another parking lot north of the boat ramps, facing the water that was calm after the snowfall the night before.

"I don't know how to start."

"I'd say the beginning. We might need to go for the short version and who's trying to kill you."

She shook her head. "That's just it. I don't know who. They tried to kill me in Amarillo and instead I took something they want back."

"Drugs?"

"No. At least I don't think it's about drugs. I grabbed a list of names and money."

"Where is it now?"

"You see, they were trying to frame me for embezzlement. I don't know how or why except that the man who ordered my death said there was no choice, that it was a direct order from the higher-ups. I grabbed the briefcase and ran."

Still keeping him at arm's length. He knew she'd deliberately not told him everything. He could hear the hesitation in her voice and recognized the deliberate selection of her words.

"How long ago was this?"

"Six very long months." She sighed and looked out the window.

"And how come they haven't found you before now? And why now?"

"I've been working as a house and pet sitter. Personal recommendations and referrals, so I don't actually work for a company."

"Off the grid. So how did they find you?"

"I've been trying to find the 'higher-ups' and have spent a lot of time searching on Brenda Ellen's computer."

Tears again. He was glad there was a seat between them. If there hadn't been, he'd probably have an arm around her shoulders or he'd be patting her back, attempting to comfort. He could relate. He'd been there. Responsible. Blaming himself. Wondering what he could have done differently.

"I never intended for anyone else to get caught up in this mess. I can't believe she's gone."

"Thing is, it *did* happen and the actions can't be changed. But you can help catch the man who strangled the life from Brenda Ellen Richardson."

"How? By going to jail? Who'll clear my name then?"

"You need to tell us everything, Bree. How can I help when you won't even trust me with your name?" He wanted to crack this case wide open. He couldn't deny the anticipation of that happening and could really get into rubbing it in his partner's face. At least for a minute or two.

Through the back window, a truck slowed and reversed. On a busy day at the lake, it might have been an innocent enough action. In the ice and snow, when the streets were basically deserted, a warning jump-started his adrenaline. It suddenly turned, speeding down the incline, and headed straight toward them.

"Hold on!" Jake threw the car into Reverse, trying to get out of the way.

Too late. The car's tires spun, barely moving them while the truck grew into the size of a monster vehicle in his side mirrors. He braced himself for the collision.

The impact slammed them forward and the truck didn't stop. Jake kept his foot on the brake, turned the wheel, pulled the emergency brake. Nothing stopped them.

"We're going into the water. Unlock the doors!"

Bree was right. The truck had the power and traction to ram them a second time, jolting them forward. There was nothing between them and the water. He pushed the button, lowering the front windows.

Dallas barked. Bree yelled. Jake released his seat belt and pulled his weapon and cell. He tossed the phone in the back. "Call 911."

Five more feet and they'd be in the lake. He released the wheel and got a firm grip on his Beretta. He turned, fired at the truck, connected. The car tipped into the water and he no longer had a shot.

"They're going to kill us."

"Stay calm. The safest place for you is here. The car's not going any farther."

"You don't know that. Get me out of here."

"Trust me, Bree. Stay here. I'll be back. I won't let anything happen to you. I promise." He tugged his heavy overcoat off. It would weigh him down in the water.

"You can't—"

Jake didn't hear the end of her sentence. The front seat was filling quickly and he had to secure the area before he got Bree out of the car. He launched himself through the passenger window and heard the gunfire before kicking hard and away from the car.

He surfaced and fired two rounds. The truck backed

away. It didn't make sense. They had the weapons to kill them. Could have rammed the car underwater completely. They were gone in seconds. No license tags to memorize and they'd probably ditch the truck a few miles away. He looked back to the car. Bree was in the front seat, calling to Dallas to come to her.

The frightened pup had crawled to the back window and wouldn't budge.

"Get to shore, Bree. Come on." He stuck his hands through the window and gently tugged on her arm.

"Oh, my gosh. She's scared to death and won't come to me." She locked eyes with him. Pleading.

"I won't leave the pup."

Bree put her cuffed hands in his and he pulled her through the window while the car shifted, sinking a bit deeper into the lake. He steadied her slim figure on the slick rocks until she could stand on her own.

He shook his head, all the while knowing he had to get the traumatized puppy. He holstered his weapon. "They might come back, so stay close to the car. I don't think it's moving again."

"Don't worry. I'm not going anywhere. You'll probably have to carry her."

The doors were still locked, keys in the ignition. He tried the lock button, electrical was gone. "Dallas, come on, pup." He tried coaxing her with kissy sounds, but like this morning at the body of Mrs. Richardson, nothing worked.

"She's blind on her right side, Detective. I don't think she can even see you."

That might partially be the reason, but most likely, the animal was just scared. As scared as the woman climbing up the grassy shore? "I told you to stay put, Bree. You keep moving and I'm coming after you instead of the dog."

"I'll be freezing in the snow instead of freezing in the water. Trust me, Detective, I have nowhere to go." She raised her cuffed wrists to him, emphasizing her captive status.

Restraints hadn't dissuaded some of the men he'd captured before. He hoped she spoke the truth because, for the life of him, he couldn't abandon the dog. He held his breath and climbed back inside the vehicle. This was the first time he'd been grateful to be issued a huge tank of a car, instead of a newer economy size.

Jake shrugged out of his suit jacket and took a couple of deep breaths to prepare for the icy submersion. He maneuvered his long body into the backseat almost as soon as his feet crossed through the window. He broke the water's surface, grabbed Dallas and then lost her when her body hit the ice water. He spun in the water to get out and caught movement on the driver's side of the car. The men who had run them into the lake were approaching through the bushes.

"Look out!" He slammed his hand against the roof, scaring the circling pup trying to get back to the dry rear window.

He pushed the dog under the water and she popped up outside the car. He followed as fast as his legs could push him through, hearing Bree's screams under the water. When he came up for air, she was still yelling at the man who carried her across his shoulder up the small hill to the road.

"Watch out!" she screamed.

He turned away from Bree's abductor and straight into something slamming into his ribs. He'd been a second too late all day, but not anymore.

The rocks were slippery under him, but he scrambled to get through the frozen reeds to the shore. He caught the piece of wood when his attacker tried to ram it in his gut. He shoved back, sending the man slipping backward on the ice.

Jake followed and got an uppercut under the man's chin. A left. Another right. The man stumbled back with each hit. Jake tugged the mask at the top of his head, showing a chin that could barely grow hair. The kid couldn't be more than twenty years old. He still held the branch in one hand while he yanked the ski mask back into place. Jake recognized the crazy, wide-eyed, out-of-his-element look.

The kid blinked, panted hard and dropped the branch. *He's going to run.* Jake was ready to dive and knock the young man to the ground, but the kid pulled a gun. He began firing—wildly. Jake heard a bullet connect with metal, and one ricocheted off a rock. And the third...

Bright shards of light exploded, obscuring his view of anything else and sending him to his knees. He hit the water, plunging face-first into the icy lake. He fought to stay aware. Bree's "no" echoed between his ears along with the thumping of his heart. There was a sharp shove against his ear. Was the floating a sensation or was he really on top of the water?

Shot. Conscious but unable to react. Was this it? Had he survived six years in a war zone to come home and drown in two feet of water?

Hell, no.

Chapter Seven

Jake was dead.

Bree would never forget the twinkle in his eyes when they first met in the diner and how he'd seemed too shy to ask for her phone number. Or how he'd rushed into the house chasing Brenda Ellen's murderer. Or how he hadn't embarrassed her in front of Julie before arresting her in the park.

A good man was dead because of her running. How many more would die? *It has to stop.* "This has to stop," she shouted into the darkness surrounding her. She sniffed one last time, rubbing her nose on her drenched, smelly coat, then kicked out against the car trunk.

Her abductors—and Jake's murderers—had been parked for several minutes. She was petrified but determined to be strong. She'd faced the unknown before. She'd faced Griffin and escaped. She could do it again with a little luck.

Footsteps. A pop. Jarring light shining in her eyes.

"Get out."

"I, um, I can't. My legs are cramping and I can't move."

"Do you think I give a flip?" As much as he tried, the man who'd shot Jake couldn't disguise that his voice was high-pitched and his eyes darted questioningly all around him. It was plain to see he wasn't in charge.

His gloved hands fisted on her collar and the handcuffs, using both to jerk her from the small trunk. Her legs protested and she fell to the concrete floor. It made no difference. He wrapped a hand in her clothing and hair at the back of her neck and dragged her across the filthy floor. He pulled her into a chair on the other side of the expansive abandoned room and began taping her to it.

The man who had carried her over his shoulder from the lake was smoking a cigarette, leaning on the roof of the compact. She wouldn't cry. Not another tear. No matter what they did to her. "You won't get away with this. The man you let drown was a homicide detective. There will be a citywide manhunt for you."

"Like anybody saw us." The younger one laughed as he sliced the end of the tape and stuck his knife back inside his boot.

"Wait," the man in charge said, flipping his cigarette into a pile of rubble. "Our little friend here must be cold in that wet coat of hers. Let me help her a minute."

"She's handcuffed, Larry. We can't—"

He waited until he was in the younger one's face and flipped open a switchblade close to his ski-mask-covered nose. "What did I say about names?"

Bree swallowed hard, her throat dry and sore from the frightened tears she'd shed as she bounced in the trunk. The blade came closer. He polished the flat side just below her collarbone, the long, sharp edge just an inch away from her throat. She dared not look down, afraid that he might cut her and everything would be over.

He guided the knife down her arm, slicing her coat like butter when he came back to her neck. Across, around, down her sleeve and slicing on the way back up. She felt the tip only a couple of times on her right arm as it snagged in her sweater. If he broke the skin, she couldn't tell in her state of mind.

He yanked the coat remnants back over her shoulders. The pieces would have fallen, but he continued, asserting his power by threatening her with each slice.

Her coat lay in shreds around the chair. The man who had shot Jake came closer and wrapped the tape around her chest, forcing her close to the chair. She could barely take a deep breath and definitely couldn't move. She could no longer tell if she shivered because of the cold or shook because of the adrenaline firing through her body.

It took her a minute after they'd both walked away, but she finally got her voice. "What are we doing here?" she yelled to the men.

The man who'd attacked Jake glanced up from the back of the car, but only for a second. He seemed nervous, young, inexperienced, while the older guy, who he'd called Larry, had that dare-me-to-hurt-you look. The same evil gleam she'd seen on Griffin's cohort's face at the animal clinic.

"What do you want?" she asked Larry and his underling. They'd ignored her since taping her to the chair. She hated not knowing why they'd kept her alive. It honestly surprised her since they'd killed Brenda Ellen in such a horrible way.

Not much time had passed since the lake. Her clothes were still wet. Each minute seemed like five while she froze in the drafty warehouse. Colder now that he'd taken so much delight in cutting her coat. Remembering the blunt side of the blade against her skin made her shiver more.

Shafts of light filtered inside from windows high above her head, too high to climb out—if she could get free. It proved the sun was still shining. But the time didn't make much difference. Not really.

No one knew where she was, and no one knew she was in danger. Jake hadn't called his department or asked for backup after he'd found her.

These men could kill her and leave her body anywhere. Her parents already thought she was dead. Absolutely no one would know. She had to get free and, if nothing else, turn herself over to the police to stop more innocent people from dying.

Jake Craig was a hero who died trying to save her. He had a family. Brenda Ellen had parents. Those families deserved the truth. Their deaths weren't going to be in vain. The tears for a man she barely knew threatened to spill, but she couldn't lose control. She'd cry later.

The two men were masked and she couldn't identify them if she did manage to escape. They'd changed cars and she'd bumped around in the trunk for a short drive across downtown.

Escaping didn't seem possible. But could she convince them to release her?

Money!

"You don't know where the money is, do you? That's why you're keeping me alive."

"Shut up. Just shut it. I won't be tellin' you again," the terrifying Larry said, punching a fist in her direction.

Facing this man was nothing like confronting Griffin in their offices. She'd been scared six months ago but able to fight. Tied and feeling helpless, she was more frightened of these men, who stood twenty feet from her. Still near the second car, they argued. Jake's murderer kept looking at his watch and then checking his cell phone.

They're waiting on instructions.

She twisted against the duct tape that barely shifted against her wet clothes. And then the handcuffs jingling made her think of Jake's body floating facedown in that water. She wanted to shriek, shout, use some of the self-defense she'd learned to hurt the man who'd killed Jake. It was an unreasonable desire, but his death seemed unreasonable, too.

She barely knew the detective, but his needless death had pushed her further than she could handle. *Get a grip on yourself and get out of here so their deaths aren't just a number!*

"You can have the money. All two million of it. You don't have to turn it over to Griffin. Have you thought of that?"

Both men stared at her. The younger started to talk, but the other hit the side of his head.

One phone call would get them their money. She'd left the briefcase with the only person from her family who knew she was alive. It would be easy to meet him—but not to save herself.

All she needed was to use one code word and her uncle would bring the police to the meeting. She might go to jail, but she was a witness to the murder of a police detective. She could put these men away for life. Jake's death would mean something.

"It's finally time," Larry said.

The younger guy dialed the phone he'd been holding. The mean one yanked it away, stormed across the warehouse and stuck it in front of her face.

"Hello, Sabrina." That smooth voice was her partner's—her former partner.

"You stinking coward. How's your leg, Griffin? Rotting off, I hope."

"I'm afraid I'm better than your policeman," he said without skipping a beat.

She swallowed hard to hold off the tears. Two people had died today because of her. She wouldn't give Griffin

Tyler the satisfaction of knowing how scared she was of these men.

The prearranged phone call confirmed what Jake had surmised about Brenda Ellen not being the intended victim. Who was she kidding? She hadn't needed any confirmation. It was her fault and she'd make up for it. Somehow.

"We have a slight problem, hon," Griffin said sweetly.

"So what?" She recognized the phony coaxing he used to talk to his clients. It had made her eyes roll six months ago. Now her stomach rolled instead.

"Always the smart aleck. We need the briefcase you stole from me."

"I don't have it."

"Look, Sabrina. These men *will* hurt you and still get their money back. So you might as well tell them."

"You don't understand. I really don't have it, Griffin. These buffoons left my stuff in the trunk of the car. Now it's with the cops—at least part of it is. The rest is hidden in Amarillo."

Hope bubbled inside her while Griffin screamed unsavory words at the masked men. "Get it back. You know what will happen if we don't. I'll instruct the others to move ahead with her family. Do whatever it takes."

Griffin disconnected and the screen went black.

"What is he talking about? What does 'move ahead with my family' mean? My family has nothing to do with the money. They can't help you. They think I'm dead."

"Too late now. Maybe you should have thought about that before you took off with the payoff." Larry flicked another cigarette over his shoulder as he shoved the other guy into a corner. He spoke too low to decipher any of the conversation.

It appeared that the men chasing her had men chasing

them. Griffin's voice hadn't just shaken with anger—he'd sounded afraid.

"Wait! I can get the money back." She could get almost all of the money from where it was hidden. But if something happened to her family… She was sinking in the deep end and needed help. Maybe she could get the police involved by exchanging the suitcase for her family. Maybe. Most likely not, but if there was a chance, she had to try. "Just let me go and I'll give you the money when I get it back."

"You said it was with the cops," the younger one whined. The mean one hit him along the side of his head again.

"Don't listen. She's going to say anything to get us to let her go," the leader said. "But it won't work."

"Do *you* want to waltz into the police station and ask for it? How do you think that will go over?" she said.

"Maybe better if you hadn't killed that cop." Larry punched the younger man standing in front of him.

Again, the thought of Detective Jake Craig being dead made her take a quick couple of breaths to stop the tears. In spite of the handcuffs, she really liked the man. He'd been smart and genuinely seemed to like Dallas.

"I keep telling you, man, I didn't kill him. The damn dog pawed at him and flipped him over. I saw the annoying SOB stand up in the water before I got in the car."

Thank you, God. Jake was okay. He was going to kill her if she escaped, but he was alive.

"I know how to get my suitcase back," she said to them. Both stared at her. Their dark eyes eerily reflected the sunlight. She wanted to gulp again but didn't allow herself. "You can exchange me for the money."

"How? I ain't calling no police station," the younger guy declared, shaking his head.

"There's a phone in my stuff. If the police have it, someone will give it to the detective and you can demand an exchange."

"What if they don't answer?"

"I don't know. Maybe someone will hear the phone ring and give Detective Craig a message. We can at least try." She wanted to plead, coax, nudge or do whatever to convince these men to get Jake involved again. He'd help. He had to help.

The man who'd carried her to the truck prodded the other. "This might be our lucky break. We still got the phone she was holding?"

"That's his," she said quickly. "He'll recognize the number straight away. Won't that help?"

"We got one shot at this. Get that phone out of the car," the mean one instructed.

The younger guy ran into the far corner of the warehouse. It was dark, but she heard the click of a door opening and saw the small pin of light from inside the car.

The one giving orders came back to her and leaned so close she could smell his rancid cologne. "You better hear what I'm about to say and understand that I'd have strangled you as quick as that other bitch if Tyler had let me. I will, if you cross us, and you probably will, anyway. No hesitation and no regret."

"If you're going to kill me, then why should I get the money back for you?"

"I know what a softie you are for them dogs you babysit. I swear to you I'll kill 'em all if I don't get that cash back." His gaze turned excited as much as his voice shook with evil delight. "Then there's your family. I could have fun watching that younger sister of yours beg a little. No tellin' what she might do first."

There was no doubt in her heart that this killer wasn't

exaggerating. He would follow through on his oath. He wanted to kill her and everyone else in his path. It didn't matter what or who. Everything about him shouted that he enjoyed killing.

"I, um, I can get you the money, but I need the phone from the police station. I hid part of it in Amarillo. But if I don't call, they'll send it to the police with a letter."

He turned away, repeating most of the words Griffin had muttered minutes before. He spun, reached out and began crushing her larynx. The tape held her upper arms close to her chest. She tried raising her hand, ineptly knocking at his side. He was going to kill her and there was nothing she could do. He squeezed just enough to keep her from getting a full breath.

"If you double-cross me, sweetheart, there's nowhere you can hide. Do you understand me? I know where your family lives, Sabrina Watkins. I don't only work for your weak-hearted vet friend. The people who call the shots are worse than you can imagine I am."

"Stop, man. Don't jump the gun. We need her." The second man pulled at the hand while she barely wheezed air into her lungs.

The madman released her and stomped away. She sucked blessed air, all the while coughing and feeling like a vise was still latched around her throat. A bottle of water was soon at her lips and tipped, pouring into her mouth. She coughed and choked, letting most of it stream down her chin.

The calm murderer wagged his finger in her face, resting the bottle on her shoulder. "Talk to your cop and convince him you're dead if he don't help. You should know my partner's not foolin' around."

Yes, she did.

"And you should also know," he whispered, "they's already got someone watching your house 24/7. As soon as they get the call, your family's sittin' in another warehouse like this one with guns at their heads. So don't think you can warn the police or nothing. 'Cause we'll know and your family's dead."

She'd been scared plenty of times over the past six months. The worst had been the day it had all started and she'd listened to them planning to kill her. This was much more horrible. If she died, that was one thing. But the maniac in the corner would seek revenge on her family, make them suffer before killing them.

She'd worried about her family's well-being before but never thought Griffin would kill them. Maybe rob their house, looking for a sign of where she was staying. It was the main reason she hadn't contacted them. Giving these monsters the money was her only choice. She couldn't let anything happen to her family.

Now she had to convince Jake to help her.

"We aren't letting you out of our sight." The mean one stormed toward them. "You tell that cop nothing. We get the phone, get rid of him—again—and we take you back to Amarillo."

"That...that won't work." Her brain scrambled for a reason and could only tell them a version of the truth. "The person who's keeping the money..."

"Yeah?"

"They...um, I convinced them to help me but I swore I'd turn the money over to the police. We need Jake to get it back."

Both men cursed. Bree shut her eyes as a fist loomed close to her head.

"Come on, man," the younger guy murmured. "She can't be beat up."

Bree opened her eyes and Larry was jerking his forearm free as he retreated to the car.

"Don't get any ideas, princess." The younger guy gently slapped her cheek. "All I want is the money. Then he can do whatever he wants."

Chapter Eight

Jake waited in a chair in Captain Kennedy's office. He was ready to face his boss, ready to explain the events of today and not look like an imbecile. He hadn't been the only detective to initially miss the dog sitter's involvement earlier in the day, yet he was the only one called back to the office to be held accountable for her kidnapping.

He'd been patient with the razing, the errands, the grunt work for his fellow detectives. He took his work seriously and would let his supervisor know that he did—even while holding a shivering puppy in the crook of his arm.

There was something special about this pup. Sad eyes. A loyal spirit. He'd connected with her this morning at the death of her owner. Giving her up wasn't an option. He'd decided to keep Dallas and wouldn't send her back to the shelter after she'd saved his life. So he held her in spite of the wet-dog smell and her shivering in her sleep. One officer at the desk had offered to take Dallas off his hands, but he'd shaken his head. Maybe his deadly look had discouraged anyone else from making another attempt.

He'd reported straight to the captain's office upon his return and had been waiting for at least half an hour. There hadn't been much for him to take care of at the scene. Owens had arrived and ordered a patrolman to escort him back. Other officers had returned and were already breaking for coffee.

"You've screwed this case up enough for a review board hearing," the captain said, slamming the door behind him and startling Dallas to a low growl. "They'll contact you when they're ready to convene. Contact your union rep, but until then, you're suspended. Your liability will be determined in regards to the escape of a prisoner and destruction of city property."

Jake stood, shifting the forty-pound pup that was getting heavier by the minute. He soothed her between the ears and used the motion to keep his own cool. He wasn't used to making mistakes. He definitely wasn't used to reprimands ending with a suspension.

"Technically, at the time, she wasn't a prisoner, just an uncooperative witness. Destruction of city property? If you mean the car, I was attacked and rammed into a lake. Doesn't that—"

Dallas interrupted him by barking, clawing at the warming blanket given to them by the paramedics.

"Don't think about setting that dog down in my office. That disgusting mutt stinks," the captain remarked before shuffling through more papers. "You should have gotten rid of it with Animal Control before reporting to me."

"Came straight here just like you requested. She saved my life, sir. I have no intention of sending her to the pound."

The captain tapped a pen, clicking the button with each touch to his desk, never looking up. Giving thought to his decision about suspending him or annoyed at the delay? Jake couldn't tell.

"I would like to explain why I—"

"Your actions today have reeked of insubordination. You disregarded direct orders and if I have any say, you'll be gone for good. I'd start looking for a job somewhere else. Maybe back in the Podunk town you sprouted from."

Again, the captain had addressed him without a direct look. The pen had waved in the air by the captain's ear, but he'd kept his gaze on the folder he'd opened. Jake swallowed hard and forced himself to loosen his hold on Dallas before he upset her further.

"I followed the lead I was assigned." Maybe Owens hadn't reported all the facts? "We'd never have known about the suspect. Or that she was the intended victim."

"So you say. If you'd followed procedures, she'd be in holding." The captain dug in his desk drawer but continued to click the pen annoyingly. "For all you know, this woman was working with the murderers and escaped."

"I saw them abduct her. We'll be lucky if she's still alive."

He slammed the drawer and finally looked Jake in the eye. "If alive, we don't need your inexperience to find her and treat her as a wanted felon." He stood, leaning forward on his desk. "Her prints match a woman who was assumed dead in an Amarillo fire. Now that we know Sabrina Watkins is alive, she's wanted for murder. But that's none of your concern."

"Assumed dead?"

"Amarillo identified her remains in the fire of her business. She's cunning and has resources enough to switch dental records. Her business partner accused her of embezzlement and the next day the building was in ashes." He sat and returned his attention to the file.

"This case feels more complicated than a murder/robbery. Are you certain—"

"You're suspended and it's no longer your concern. Leave your badge." The man didn't bother looking him in the eye while suspending him. He dialed the phone and requested Personnel.

Reprimands were never easy to take. Mistakes were made and corrected. You looked the commanding officer in the eye like a man, assuring him you understood. With your salute, you assured him you'd learn from your error and it wouldn't happen again. But what did you do when a man refused to look at you?

Jake reached for the door with his free hand. *This isn't the military, but I still don't retreat,* he thought to himself.

"If given the opportunity, I'd be a good Dallas homicide detective." An unlikely harrumph surfaced from behind him. Jake pivoted in time to receive the older man's glare.

"There are plenty of officers who put in their time and are waiting for a chance in this department. They know how we do things and have more experience guarding our citizens." He looked back at the paperwork on his desk, using the pen to point to a table by the door. "Leave your badge and weapon."

"Can't help you with that. Must be at the bottom of the lake with the car." His biceps burned from holding the pup in his arms, but denying the captain his moment re-energized his determination not to complain.

"Incompetent fool."

Jake's badge *was* in the car, inside his coat pocket, nothing foolish about its location. His weapon, however, was in the small of his back, under his suit jacket. Keeping his firearm did amount to insubordination. It belonged to him and he wouldn't give it up. His instincts told him he'd be needing it to save Bree Watkins.

Oorah.

He'd halfway decided to help her when she'd cried into the pup's fur just before they'd been forced into the lake. Now that he was suspended there was no question. His gut told him she was in trouble and someone had to help. If she was still alive, he'd find her and straighten this mess out.

Never leave a man behind.

"I put in my time, Captain. Eight years to be exact. Six of them overseas in a war zone. If there weren't a lady present..." He shifted Dallas, who barked on cue. "I might have shown you a bit of the experience I obtained guarding our citizens."

If there'd been a chance of being reinstated, it was none to gone now. The slamming door sent the remaining people in their office running. He stomped to his desk like a sullen child, again upsetting the pup. He nuzzled her with his chin before tying her to his chair.

Alone, he stowed his few personal items in the same box that he'd brought them to the office the previous week. Dallas patiently waited, wrapped in the remnants of the emergency blanket, her sleepy eyes drooped to a close for another nap. He could relate; it had been a long day.

An annoying cell phone rang. Muted, like in a desk. He ignored it and finished stowing his things. He sat on the corner of his desk, scrubbing his face and wondering what he could do to find Sabrina Watkins. Nothing official. That was for certain. He'd made no friends at the station. With the exception of Sharon in Forensics. He'd asked for a heads-up about the fingerprints, but—shoot, he didn't have his phone.

"That's it, Dallas." The pup's head sprung up at her name. "I can trace my phone. Bree or her abductors might still have it."

The annoying cell tune played again. Another look around the desks and he saw the screen light up inside an evidence bag. It was part of the contents from Bree's suitcase.

Late on a Saturday afternoon, there had been few officers at the station. He took a step toward the break room to locate the officer handling the evidence. *What if they miss the call? What if it's her?*

The only person in sight was the captain, who had his ear to the phone, back to his door. By the looks of it, he was shouting and ticked off—probably because Jake had dared to question his authority. Telling him the suspect's phone was ringing would do what? Would he listen to reason? Send someone to rescue her?

Jake lifted the evidence bag. It could be anyone calling her. Anyone from her life, leaving a message or a clue to what was really going on.

Hell, that's my number calling.

No retreat. He broke the seal and answered.

"Who is this and why do you have my phone?"

"Jake. Thank God, you're alive and okay. I can't believe it's you."

Bree's voice sounded relieved but nervous. He'd encountered numerous hostile witnesses afraid for their lives. He recognized the vocal patterns. He thought he'd been finished with surprises today.

"Where are you, Miss Watkins? Can you talk? Do you know who abducted you?" He lowered his voice and moved back to his desk, keeping a close eye on the doorway and stuffing the evidence bag into a file cabinet.

"They want the money located in my suitcase, Jake. If you'll bring it to Brenda Ellen's house, they promise to let me go."

A quick glance showed him there wasn't enough money to kill over. A couple of hundred had already been bagged. Something was off. "I don't know what you're talking—"

Bree screamed. It sounded like she'd been slapped and the phone had fallen to the floor.

"You bring the suitcase where we met this mornin' or you'll find another dead dog walker," a man shouted.

"Wait, there's nothing—"

The line was dead.

No one in the station had witnessed the call and the captain was still occupied with his own conversation. Jake slipped the phone into his jacket pocket. The suitcase had been emptied. Mostly personal items. Clothes, a toiletry bag and dark hair dye—making him wonder about the natural color of Bree's hair.

Constantly scanning for the officer's return, he quickly searched the lining of the case. Nothing.

Then he dumped the toothpaste and makeup from the smaller bag. A lining had been sewn inside. A little tug and it was gone. Hidden between two pieces of cardboard was a large stack of hundred-dollar bills. He stuck all of it in his pocket and replaced the personal items to cover his discovery.

No time to count. He scooped Dallas under one arm and the box in the other, then left the building.

What the heck are you doing, man? Put the money back before someone notices. You're breaking your oath to uphold the law. Are you keeping your promise to a dead woman? Or did the amethyst eyes take over more than your brain?

He didn't have to think about it. Bree Watkins was innocent and needed his help. If his gut was wrong, he'd be the one dumping her in his captain's lap along with her two buddies who'd sent the department car into White Rock Lake.

Inside his truck, the questions of how he'd accomplish this feat without assistance crossed his mind a time or two. A rescue with no team. No backup. No plan.

"Aw, don't be scared, pup. Come here, girl." He patted his leg and Dallas crawled onto his lap, swiveling her head to view him from her left. "There's always the marine corps if I don't go to jail. Either way, I'll get you a good home."

But before that, he had to find Bree. He'd seen the desperation for someone to believe her in those special eyes. He felt the setup in his gut. It was all too convenient. Her genuine look of hopelessness as that brawny son of a bitch carried her away strengthened his resolve to get her back. If they'd wanted her dead, they would have shot her in the lake.

There had to be something he was missing. They knew he was a cop. The stack of bills wasn't enough to risk a ransom drop. There had to be more to the story. He needed details from Bree.

The phone company didn't want to cooperate, but he coaxed until they verified his phone was near the Lakewood area. He'd make good time back to the murder scene. Bree's abductors wouldn't know what he drove so he passed by the house, parking diagonal with a good view of the perimeter. The sky had darkened while the sun dropped behind more forecasted snow clouds. He waited a good fifteen minutes. No activity anywhere on the street.

Dallas whined when he moved her off his lap. She was probably hungry, thirsty and needed to pee. But she'd have to wait in the rear seat of his truck. He had a single-handed rescue to execute.

Chapter Nine

Bree's captors had taped her to the dining room chair in the same way they had at the warehouse. Brenda Ellen's home was eerily empty. She didn't know why she'd hoped police or anyone else would have been here. Her friend and employer had mentioned that her parents had retired to the Hill Country near Llano, Texas, and they didn't travel long distances.

"Remember what I told you. We'll be close by. If your cop buddy thinks about throwing you in jail, he's dead. Then we start on your family. We'll be watching." The man who'd choked Brenda Ellen was dangerously crazy and determined to get the money. He would have killed anyone here.

Somehow, she had to convince Jake to take her to Amarillo. No, she could get to her uncle on her own. She just needed her phone to call, then Uncle Jerry would know it was okay to give her the money. *Please have the money, Jake.* She'd been instructed to leave with the cop, bring him with her and prevent him from seeking help from other cops. Maybe she could escape if the keys to the car were still in the kitchen. She could borrow Brenda Ellen's car without the police realizing it was missing.

Jake didn't have to help her. He was safer if he didn't. Now that she had a plan, waiting was miserable. Her wrists were sore, her legs weak. She had eaten only two fries since she'd met Jake that morning at the diner. Even then it had only been some toast and coffee to tide her over until she could cook her own here.

This morning seemed so long ago.

The interior of the house was pitch-black. The blinds and drapes covered the windows. It had been different this morning, full of light and the promise of a soft bed for two weeks. Bree wanted to cry, recalling once again that Brenda Ellen was gone.

No, she hadn't just died. She'd been violently murdered. Her own throat ached, her stomach growled again and she desperately needed water. At the moment there was nothing to do except think and pray. She heard the click of a doorknob turning in the silence of the empty house.

"Detective Craig?" Her whisper came out dry and hoarse.

He silently moved through the kitchen and dining room doorway, raising a finger to his lips to silence her. Then he replaced his hand under his handgun. She'd seen actors imitate "clearing the room," as they put it. Experiencing a strong man like Jake coming to rescue her sort of made her insides jump around like an excited Chihuahua.

"They left right after they phoned you. We're alone." Did she sound convincing? She didn't want to get him killed. Two souls on her conscience were enough.

"Are you injured?" he whispered, kneeling at her side with his back to her, weapon ready to defend.

Natural posture for a police officer. It wasn't just for her. *Remember that.* She'd been so alone, having dreamed too often that someone would swoop into the picture and save her. The delight that he'd come to her rescue stemmed from that wishful thinking—not reality. He was just doing his job.

"No." She cleared her parched throat. "I'm a little shaky, but what about you? I thought he'd killed you. I just need you to cut me loose and we can get out of here. Did Dallas stay with you? Is she back at the animal shelter?"

He didn't acknowledge her. He stood and pressed his back to the wall next to the staircase. There was a stark white bandage just above his ear. He must have sliced it when he'd fallen into the lake.

Poor little Dallas. The thought of the puppy roaming in the snow saddened her heart.

She remained silent while he searched the house. There was no way for her to prove they were alone. The crazy murderer could have returned to the house, lying in wait to kill them both. She wouldn't put it past him. Her only hope was that those men needed the money and knew they wouldn't recover it if they killed her.

"The house looks clear," he said as he stepped from the stairs. His gun disappeared behind his back and he pulled his pocketknife, slicing through the silver tape strapping her in place.

"I hope you have the key to these." She jangled the cuffs, hearing them clink in the dark. "A girl loves jewelry, but this is a little much."

She couldn't get to Amarillo if she was handcuffed. *Please have the key.*

"Good to see you haven't lost your sense of humor. The cuffs stay until I get some satisfactory answers. I've already broken enough laws without freeing a wanted fugitive trying to escape."

"Wanted fugitive?"

"Dallas P.D. wants you for questioning about your employer's murder. Along with this business of identity theft, embezzlement and arson. Then there's the body Amarillo P.D. assumed was you when your business burned." Dark brown eyes, even darker now, kept searching the room and sliding to the door to the backyard, watching for the enemy. If he knew what these men were capable of, he'd want to leave as quickly as possible.

"Shouldn't you be reading me my rights or something? If that's the case, I may as well ask for a lawyer now."

His eyes narrowed, bringing his brows into a straight line. "But I didn't Mirandize you."

Her eyes had adjusted to the dark long before his arrival. She noticed the sharp angles making up his intense face. "What does that mean?"

"I'd like to hear what happened directly from you before I make up my mind. Right now I think we should get someplace safe."

Nowhere was safe until the money was back in Griffin's grubby paws. Jake lifted her to her numb legs, continuing to hold her elbow when she stumbled, encouraging her to the edge of the kitchen.

"Wait. Please. Did you bring the phone and the money from my suitcase?"

He shook his head and she couldn't breathe. It was worse than being choked. And just like that, her knees were on the carpeted floor. Tears blurred her vision and she couldn't prevent the incoherent babbling about thinking he was dead or getting him killed. It all ran together in her head and especially across her lips.

"No one's going to harm you," Jake said, now on his knee beside her. "I can call for backup. You're safe now."

"We can't go out there yet." She shook her head and took hold of his hand. "Please don't." She lowered her voice to a whisper so they couldn't be heard. "If they can't kill you or me…they'll kill my family." There was no doubt in her mind everyone she loved was in danger. No one would be safe. "They want their money back."

He leaned in close to her ear. "I assume they're listening. Just remember I'm on your side. How much did you steal?"

"I didn't—" Jake knew they were listening. "That monster will kill anyone who gets in his way. He likes hurting and killing. I have to get Griffin the rest of the money and I need my phone to get it. You have to help me, Jake."

Jake wanted them to hear what they said. She could see it in his eyes and the slight nod of his head.

"I need more than that you feel threatened, Bree," he said louder. "Do you want to have this conversation here? Okay. Who are these men? Where did they take you? Why does the Amarillo P.D. think you're dead? What's so important about this particular phone? There's nothing stored on it. I checked."

"I must use that number to call the person who has the money. If I use any other phone, he won't come. There aren't any exceptions. No one will ever find the money." She covered her face with her cold hands. The handcuffs jingling snapped her attention back to Jake before she spilled all her secrets.

Stay calm. Griffin's men already knew too much. Then what would they do? Force her to make a call to her uncle on the off chance they wouldn't kill everyone she loved? If the deep furrow between Jake's brows meant he was confused, that was good. She'd almost told him her uncle's name.

"Let me get you somewhere safe and you can start from the beginning. Maybe I'll actually understand some of this," he said, lifting her to her feet and guiding her to the door.

"Do you have a way to get the phone, Jake?"

"That might be possible." He gently tugged, attempting to get her outside—she stayed put. "You told me to bring the money from your case, but there was only a few grand. Not enough to kill over."

"I only brought one bundle for emergency. I think there was around two million in the briefcase. I didn't stop to count. I was in a hurry at the time."

"No wonder they want the money back. Let's go." He twisted at his waist and took another look around the room. "You need police protection while they sort this mess out."

"I can't go to jail." His gun was right at her fingers. She knew how to use it. She didn't want to hurt or betray him—he'd already sacrificed so much for her. But she couldn't let him take her to the police. He wouldn't believe her story. Why would they? She sounded crazy and just didn't have a choice.

"It's better if we sort through—"

The gun shook in her hands. She was more afraid she'd pull the trigger by accident than what would happen if he took it away. The straight edge of his hand chopped hard on her wrist, numbing her fingers, which dropped his weapon. He snatched it before she had feeling again.

"Weren't you ever taught not to play with loaded guns. Don't be foolish, Miss Watkins." He stashed the pistol behind him again.

"I think you'd try to get away if it were your family they were threatening," she said, to focus her thoughts on what was important.

"I wouldn't try. I'd succeed. Are they threatening your family, Bree?"

He held out his hand and she placed both of hers in his grasp. He pulled her close, wrapping an arm around her waist, keeping her on her feet. Still cuffed, her hands were between them, separating their chests. She could feel the rapid beating of her heart and his. She didn't miss the sharp intake of his breathing as her body connected with his.

His eyes had dropped to her breasts. Her nipples—hard from a damp bra and the cold—poked through the thin cotton turtleneck. Any man would have taken a look, right? Her coat and sweater had been sopping wet. The man who'd thrown her over his shoulder had scared her half to death by using a knife as long as her hand to hack the coat off her arms since the handcuffs were in the way.

How could she be so aware of everything around her and so unfocused where her family was concerned?

"Hired thugs are on their way to abduct my family in Amarillo right now. If I don't get the money to them in three days, the man you fought with is going to kill my little sister. They could be hurting them already. Please don't put their lives in danger by taking me to jail."

"Let's go."

"Jake, please," she begged. It was the only option left for her. "Please give me the phone and let me go."

He yanked her closer. "Why don't you tell me the truth?"

She tugged his shirt collar until he bent low enough to get her lips close to his ear, then she whispered, "They're listening to us through a phone that's taped to the edge of the table. If we don't prove that I have the cash, we're both dead. Right now. They told me not to say anything or they'd shoot you. I swear."

His warm breath brushed her ear, sending the wrong type of message to her body, before he whispered, "Trust me, Bree. I can get you out of here safely, but you can't lie to me again."

Jake stood tall, giving her a moment for her head to catch up to his words. It had been so long since she'd been this close to a man… No, wait, she was light-headed from dehydration, lack of sleep and too much stress. The adrenaline of being abducted and rescued was doing weird things to her insides. Jake Craig had nothing to do with it.

He glared intently through the sliding door into the darkness of the backyard. "It goes against my better judgment," he said firmly, loud enough to be heard. "I'm already in hot water with the captain. I took some of the money that was with the phone."

He put a finger over her lips. Then slipped his hand into his pocket and showed her the money she'd hidden in her bag. He removed several bills and slapped them onto the dining table. "I could only grab a couple of thousand or they'd realize something was wrong with the inventory."

"You're going to help me?"

"Nothing's holding me here. I can help you get past the cops and protect you from the men who abducted you. I just want a piece of the action. Have we got a deal?"

If she hadn't known it was all an act, she might have been fooled. The quirk of his eyebrow and the slight rise of the corner of his mouth would have convinced her he was sincere and just in it for the money.

But after the day they'd shared, she knew this man was much too honorable to succumb to a bribe.

Thank goodness the men listening at the other end of the phone had no clue.

Chapter Ten

Jake didn't let go of her as they left the house. Greeted by Dallas at the truck window, Bree's face lit up. He unlocked his truck door, ready to let her scoot across the seat. Instead, she faced him, blowing on her fingers, her dark eyes darting around as if she was thinking hard on her next words.

"I need to call my family as soon as possible," she finally said.

"I need more information before I allow you to call anyone. Get in."

"Hi, Dallas." Bree's voice changed. No longer sounding worried, she made kissy noises and leaned across the seat to pet the dog.

The pup left the warmth of the emergency blanket stretching from seat to seat, trying to get to his suspect. Bree lifted her, kissing the pup between her ears. He'd acted the same way while the captain handed down his suspension. Rubbing those silky ears between his fingers, the news just hadn't felt as bad.

The officers he'd been working with resented his promotion, but he'd screwed up more than a couple of times today. So maybe he'd been expecting bad news from the captain. Just not a suspension.

Jake took his notebook, which had been drying in

the cup holder, and wrote "R U bugged," then showed it to Bree.

"No. They were using one of their cells on speaker-phone to listen. He said they'd be watching through binoculars."

He pulled the phone from the console and began to dial.

"What are you doing?"

"Calling the police to pick these guys up. They've got to get inside the house again if they intend on grabbing their phone."

Bree hit the cell from his hand and it tumbled to his feet. "If these two are caught, there are more in Amarillo to do the killing."

"What the hell are you involved in? Drug running? What money are they talking about?" His hands shook a bit. He was tired, but he'd noticed the tremor had shown up more this past week with the additional stress of the promotion.

"I've been trying to figure that out for six very long months. Are you okay, Jake? You look kind of weird."

"What?"

"I said, I've been thinking it has something to do with money laundering. But I have no idea what."

He popped his neck, relaxing, preventing the anxiety or stress from interfering with his work. "Did you get a look at their faces? Any chance you can identify them? Do you remember the vehicles they used today? Anything special about where they held you?"

"Can you interrogate me after we get moving, Jake? It's freezing in here." She brought her hands under her chin, shivering. "They're also watching. Remember?"

He'd noticed at the house she'd been cold and hadn't given it a second thought. He'd been too busy making the decision to cross yet another line for this woman. Why was he trusting her and willing to deceive the very men he'd been working with hours before? Did it go back to the attraction he'd felt at the diner? It couldn't be. There's no way he'd give everything up again for a woman. Just no way.

"Sorry." He cranked his truck, turned the heater to high and jerked his jacket from his shoulders to drape around her. "What happened to your coat and gloves?"

"They were wet and he...um, the one called Larry, cut off my coat." Her voice changed as if she'd made up her mind to say something that wasn't the complete truth. "I'd be warmer if I could put my arms through the sleeves." She shook her latched wrists in his direction, then dropped them back to cradle the pup in her lap.

"I've got a key at my apartment." *And police headquarters and in my pocket.* "We should call 911 and leave an anonymous tip that we saw strangers at the crime scene. That sort of thing. At least let the department know something's up. They might get prints this time."

"Please, Jake. We can't do that. Somehow, they'll make sure we go to Amarillo. If I don't, they'll kill my family. Are you taking me there? Will it cause you more problems?"

"I was suspended today and have broken several laws in the past couple of hours. I don't seem to be too concerned about causing myself problems."

"Suspended because of me? But you're the one who found me and— Why would they suspend a good detective?"

"It's complicated. This murder was actually my first and last case for the Dallas P.D. Your turn to share some details about what's going on."

"I'm so sorry that I've wrecked your life."

"You don't get to wear that title, Bree. My ex-wife claimed it a while back."

She covered her face with her hands, acting ashamed. "Have I endangered even more people? Do you have kids?"

He shook his head, glad for the first time in years that he and Jennifer hadn't pursued children. He hadn't wanted to be an absentee father. And now, if they had, he'd wonder if they were even his.

The more pressing issue was to get Sabrina Watkins to tell him the entire story. Start to finish—or near finish. It was clear she didn't trust him enough to share yet. She kept dodging his questions.

It was a long drive to Amarillo and eventually he'd get it out of her. *Gain her trust. Then you can help and maybe get your job back or some other type of employment.*

"You were flying under the radar by house-sitting. That was a good idea with characters like that searching for you. You'll need new civvies and a coat before we hit the road."

The snowfall was heavy again. He'd listened to the weather off and on today. Dallas wouldn't see much more, then the temperature would warm up and most of the roads would be clear by late morning.

"I appreciate everything you've done. You've saved my life twice today. But after you take these handcuffs off, don't you think I should leave? You shouldn't get more involved. It's already cost you your job and almost your life. Maybe you could exaggerate my escape abilities and let your supervisor think I conked you on the head or something."

He rubbed the lump under the bandage on the right side of his head where he'd been "conked" for real that afternoon. He hadn't meant to draw her attention to it, but her intake of breath and immediate touch proved he had.

"What happened to your head? Did you hit it on something?"

"The bullet grazed me. If it hadn't been for the pup

pawing at my ear, I might have completely passed out and drowned." He watched for a vehicle that might be tailing them. Those two goons might try to follow, but he was determined not to be a step behind this time.

"You've been shot and suspended and it's all my fault." She dropped her forehead to the passenger window.

He could only see her shoulder and matted hair. "I think we need to clean up before we drive five or six hours. Even Dallas is smelling like a sewer."

"Do you think that's a good idea? They could be right behind us."

"I've been driving in circles to make sure we weren't followed. We're clear. My apartment is just around the corner." He wouldn't gain her trust if she knew he'd been close to taking her to the police station. Dang if he knew why he'd changed direction. "Tell me about Dallas. Why would anyone adopt a half-blind dog?"

"You've met her." She raised the head of the pup and kissed her fur. "First, she's absolutely adorable and doesn't let the blindness slow her down at all. I volunteered at the shelter and introduced Brenda Ellen to her after she lost her first dog. She brought her home the next day."

"So you really like dogs." He slowed the truck for the last stop light before his complex.

Bree didn't allow the handcuffs to encumber her. He watched her stroke the black fur, keeping Dallas calm and silent. His dad always said you could tell a man's true character by how he treated his animals. If that were true about this woman…maybe it was the reason he'd sided with her.

"I'm glad you kept her," she said softly.

He parked at the rear of his lot with easy access to leave in a hurry. He'd half expected that his fellow officers would have the place surrounded. He'd stolen evidence in order to save this woman's life.

"Listen." He held her arm through his jacket and she raised those violet eyes questioningly at him. "Stealing evidence isn't the most honorable thing I've done. Probably not the most dishonorable, either."

"You're saving my family. What could be dishonorable about that?"

His mind was made up and he needed to be honest. "You've got two choices. Either go to jail now. Or turn the rest of the money and evidence over to me and go to jail in Amarillo."

She sat straighter, stiff, looking petrified. "I see."

"I'm a cop. What did you really expect?"

Almost spilling Carl's coffee and the woman who had shyly giggled at his awkwardness seemed like a distant memory. *Be honest.* Okay, his physical attraction to Bree had influenced his decisions earlier in the day. But he couldn't admit that to her. He could barely admit it to himself.

"I'm not certain," she whispered. "A lot's happened today that I was unprepared for and I'm so tired it's hard to think straight. I don't want anyone else to get hurt."

"We'll make certain your family's safe. It'll work out, Bree."

"I'm sure you think so."

"I'll be with you the entire time. Nothing will happen to you, but I need to know everything."

"I understand. Now? Or can we go inside first?"

They got out of the truck. Dallas was in Bree's arms and he wrapped his jacket around her. She shrugged it away, along with his arm as he tried to take the forty pounds of Lab to his door.

Inside, she set Dallas on the floor, untied the makeshift silver leash and held her hands out for him to remove the cuffs. He reached into his pocket for the key and a sound of disgust escaped her lips.

"I could have lied to you about why I'm taking you to Amarillo," he said as he pocketed the cuffs again.

"Thanks for reminding me that I'm a fugitive. I know what to expect now." She rubbed her wrists and then pointed down the hall. "Is the bathroom this way?" He nodded and she ran the short distance. Hand on the knob, she hesitated. "Do you need to come in with me?"

"It has to be this way, Bree. I promised to uphold the law." He'd sworn several oaths over his lifetime. Did he still believe he could keep all of them?

Her hands dropped against her sides as she faced him, visibly defeated. He hated what he had to do, what she must think of him. He admitted, "I don't have a choice."

"Neither do I. No one ever asked me if destroying my life was okay. They didn't ask if I wanted to give up everything I'd ever known. Or if I wanted to lose my family and have them think I was dead. And they didn't ask if it was okay to blow up my business and destroy everything I'd worked for since high school. I'm hiding from men who want to kill me for the reason that I was a convenient scapegoat. I completely understand about not having a choice."

He could argue with her, but why? Because he'd wanted her phone number that morning? That path was off-limits now. Why? Maybe she was the first woman inside his apartment since the divorce. So what? Maybe he'd brought her here because he couldn't let her out of his sight.

Again, so what? She was an attractive woman who he happened to be helping with a problem.

Stop lying. She's a suspect who might be as guilty as those men who'd abducted her. How was he lying to himself? A victim of circumstances or a lying con artist? Did it matter? No more questions. No more ifs. He'd save the Watkins family or put Bree in jail.

Across the room, Dallas circled as if she was about to curl up and sleep. "I should probably walk you before you settle down." The pup squatted instead. Too late again. He was finished being a step behind. Time to act like who he was.

A marine.

Chapter Eleven

"If you're hungry, I make a mean hot turkey, pastrami and Swiss sandwich." Jake had his head in the fridge. There wasn't much else to offer. A cold beer wasn't exactly what a freezing woman should drink. He didn't even have frozen dinners left to heat and serve. He'd been guzzling the coffee swill at the department for a week, avoiding the grocery store, occasionally getting a good cup from a diner.

Bree's soggy shoes squeaked on the worn linoleum. "Are you certain staying here long enough to eat is a good idea? They said they'd be watching us until we had the money. I don't think stopping off for a change of clothes and a hot sandwich is what they had in mind."

He checked his watch, eight o'clock. He hoped MacMahan could get the gear together in two hours. He needed a list and a moment alone. That's all the time they could spare before they should be on the road. "I have to make a quick call."

"When can I call my family?"

"It might not be a brilliant idea, but we both stink to high heaven because of that lake dunking. I don't plan to ride in that truck with you for five or six hours in these clothes. Now, are you hungry? I happen to be starved." He pulled the sandwich stuff from the shelf, then pulled the skillet from the dish drain, keeping an eye on his frustrated prisoner.

Bree Watkins glared at him as she crossed her arms and headed toward a kitchen chair. "Dallas and I don't have a problem with the smell."

Dipping the knife in the butter, he acknowledged that she wouldn't let the call to her family wait for long. He also realized an exasperated sigh had come from him. Her family could be in danger or they could be the ones behind everything. He had no way of knowing and needed time to weigh his options. Time to think of a plan instead of react to the problem.

He'd ignore the request for a phone call until he made a decision. Turning from the bread, he pointed the butter tub in Bree's direction. "I'm in charge and I do have a problem with smell. That's a brand-new truck sitting out there. And we really do stink. Now strip."

"I beg your pardon?" Her shock erupted as a nervous giggle.

The same cute sound from early that morning that had been so damn attractive. *Stow it, marine.* One more time, he debated sharing why it was important to wait on the supplies he needed. He'd be prepared this time.

"I'll wash your clothes while you shower. How did you think we were going to clean up?"

"I… That can't possibly be a good idea. What if they come here and I'm—"

"Soapy?" He laughed, unable to stop himself. The look on her face was priceless. "We weren't followed. Promise. If you're worried about getting on the road, you should probably get moving."

She stood and Dallas jumped off the couch to follow. Bree picked her up and Jake held out his hands to take her.

"I'm serious about the stench. The paramedics warned

me about an infection." He pointed to his bullet graze. "Do it for me. After all, I did save your life."

"I can't believe you're trying to guilt me into compliance. Oh, my gosh! Hanging around here can't be a good idea." His "prisoner" huffed down the short hallway. He and Dallas followed close behind. He got his hand on the door, stopping her from closing it. Guilty conscience or not, it seemed to do the trick.

"What now?" she asked, facing him, trying to close the door. "You are not coming in this bathroom with me."

"I need your clothes and you aren't locking me out."

"In your dreams, Detective. I am not taking my clothes off in front of you." Her words were commanding, but she took a step in retreat when he cupped his hand around the door.

"You can hop behind the curtain and hand them to me before you turn the water on. Nothing lecherous about that."

"I, um, I'm not sure I trust you that much."

He crossed his arms like she had in the kitchen and made himself comfortable leaning against the doorjamb, keeping the door open with his foot. Hoping that he looked innocent, with no ulterior motive. In reality his thoughts were just like any other red-blooded marine when confronted with the possibility of a naked woman. To make the situation worse, he'd been attracted to Bree since the first shy giggle drawing his attention to the corner of the diner.

If today hadn't happened, finding her would be a primary objective. But right now, his objective was to get them cleaned up, gather some gear and be gone.

Bree toed off her wet shoes. Funny, he was supposed to be a detective and hadn't noticed that she'd been wearing a tight-fitting sweater all day. Purple, close to the color of her eyes. Granted, she'd been in a heavy coat most of the time. But in the bathroom light, her eyes were the deep amethyst he'd admired first thing.

Dallas sat on the floor between them. He picked her up and took a long sniff of the puppy. "You smell terrible. That lake water left all of us stinky grimy. You have to clean up, too, girl. Now don't look at me with those sad, puppy-dog eyes. It won't be so bad."

"It's completely embarrassing and wrong. I haven't known you twenty-four hours and this is… I'd never do this."

"You're taking a shower and we're doing nothing improper. I'll keep my eyes closed. See?" He clamped his eyes shut, concentrating on sounds.

The shower curtain holders slid opened and closed. Her body shifted. Even if he opened his eyes, he'd only see her silhouette behind his cheap blue curtain. He assumed the wet jean material was being peeled from each slender thigh and tiny foot. Yeah, she had feet the appropriate size for someone of her short height. The plastic shifted again, a plop on the bath mat. Then the purple sweater dropped from over the rod.

It would be wrong to open his eyes and watch the rest.

What's wrong were the images in his head. Actually, there was nothing wrong with the images there. After being loyal to his wife and being stationed overseas for six years, his imagination was pretty darn good. Naked, sleek muscles with water droplets hugging every curve…

Eyes open, he put the pup on the floor and bent to scoop her clothes into a pile, immediately wishing he could throw them away instead of wasting time in the wash cycle. The shower came on. His body reacted. A woman he was attracted to was on the other side of that curtain.

She's my prisoner. Sort of my prisoner. I'm not a cop anymore.

He couldn't lie. He wanted Sabrina Watkins with a fierce part of himself he hadn't dealt with in a very long time.

The curtain moved again. The pup had nudged it aside. He saw the outline of Bree bend at the waist to help her inside the tub.

"So you decided on a bath, too? Good girl."

"Clean towel is on the hanger." He pointed to the rod over the toilet. "My robe's on the back of the door when you're done."

"I'll only be a few minutes."

"Great."

There wasn't a window in the bathroom and probably no way for Bree to escape while his back was turned—especially naked—but he couldn't risk it. She had managed to get past him twice today, not including the abduction. He marched to the kitchen, dropped the stinky clothes and obtained a screwdriver from under the sink, where he kept a small tool kit.

Removing the doorknob only took a couple of minutes. He was silent enough that he didn't think Bree heard him. Bright laughter from the shower in spite of the desperate way she must feel made him wish she really was the first *woman* in his shower instead of the first prisoner.

As soon as she finished in the shower, he'd start the washer. He got everything ready, and noticed how tattered the sweater was. Unlike the jeans, which looked barely worn. It didn't make sense. *Dammit.* She'd said he'd cut the coat off. He'd sliced her sweater and she hadn't said a thing.

Not one word. And he'd forced her into a shower without thinking about any possible trauma she might be suffering from the abduction. He dialed a number he hadn't been able to dial in months.

Mac had been a marine specialist and a good friend who

mustered out three months before him. Jake didn't know if he'd answer with only an exchange of phone numbers over the past two years.

"Hey, Craig, buddy. Where have you been keeping your lonesome self?"

"It has been a while, Mac. I'm texting you a shopping list."

"For girls? I've been waiting for this. I heard you got divorced." His friend laughed.

"Afraid you're going to continue to wait for that party. You still in private security and able to supply friends?" He walked to the bathroom, wanting to push the door open and...and what? The shower was still running. He could hear a few words addressed to the dog.

"How long do I have to fill the order?" Mac asked.

Jake pivoted to the kitchen, away from Bree. "ASAP. I'd like wheels up by 2200."

"You'll be limited to what I have on hand and how long it takes me to get to wherever you live. You need a clean vehicle?"

"I'm good on that front. Something's better than nothing. I'll text you the address."

"Thought you had a whole police force at your back, man."

"Yeah, not so much. The quicker the better." Bree's clothes were pretty ruined. His blood boiled. The rips in the back of her sweater were probably from that psycho cutting her coat off. And he'd seen the small wounds on her right arm. *Son of a bitch.*

"One more thing, Mac. There are a few items for a friend. No laughing. No questions. Shop anywhere that's open."

"You need any help with this op, Jake?"

"Not this go-round, man. This is something I have to

do on my own." He couldn't let anyone else risk anything. He didn't know why he thought he could trust this woman, but he couldn't ask anyone else to.

"Okay, but you'll owe me a favor sometime and you better plan on departing at 2230."

"Not ever a problem. Thanks, Mac." He disconnected and texted the list he'd been mentally preparing. He also flipped on the Weather Channel, hoping they'd rotate through what the weather was like in the Texas Panhandle. The snow front had come from the northwest all week, but he hadn't heard anything about the forecast.

"Jake, I need you." She couldn't mean what first entered his mind.

He dropped the phone and sprinted to the bathroom, curious. The wet dog aroma hit him as soon as he entered the misty shower and he knew why she'd called for help. Bree contained a shivering Dallas next to her in the tub.

It was hard to concentrate on anything other than her creamy skin that had a dozen or so freckles. She had excellent muscle tone. Just right for a woman, proving that she worked out somewhere. Wishing that was all he could see, he focused on the squirming dog with a paw on the edge of the tub instead of the perfect derriere covered by one layer of terry cloth.

"She's through playing, but I still need to rinse my hair. You forgot to leave extra towels."

Bree was wrapped in one of the four that he owned. He held his hands out but was met with a vigorous shake of dog and tiny shocked squeal from Bree. He needed to act fast, before that corner holding her towel in place became unsecured and he could see more than he needed. Or should.

"Are you going to wrap her in your dirty shirt?" Her

perfect lips raised in a clever smile. "You wouldn't want her to get *stinky* again. Would you?"

"Just a sec." The clean towels were still in the dryer. He grabbed them and got back in the tiny bath just as Dallas jumped from the tub and began shaking.

He dropped the towel on top of the pup and rubbed. "What's the idea?"

"I had to set her down. My towel was slipping. Then she jumped. Watch out, she's slippery when wet."

Slippery tile was much easier to handle than the slippery slope that would happen if he caught a glimpse of more than bare shoulders and knees. There's no telling where he—or they—might fall.

Bed was the most probable conclusion.

Chapter Twelve

Bree stared at Jake's king-size bed. It looked inviting and absolutely huge. Since he'd barely let her out of his sight, she was stuck standing in the hall alternating her view between bed and bath. It was either envying Dallas, sound asleep and curled in the middle of a large mattress with soft pillows, or Jake's jean-clad backside as he dried the tile with a washcloth since he was out of towels.

Sometimes the bath view made her forget she was in trouble or that the man on his knees had threatened to turn her in to the police. Duh, he *was* the police. He'd changed his dirty slacks for an old pair of work jeans. Slung low on his hips, frayed holes in both knees and, of course, no shirt.

She tightened the belt around her only garment and switched to staring at the bed. His fluffy robe was nice and warm for all of her body except her feet. Those were covered with a pair of his woolen socks that looked and felt like marine issue.

"Don't you have a pair of sweats I could put on? You could shower and we could be on our way in fifteen minutes instead of a couple of hours waiting on clothes."

"I told you—"

"I know, you've got it covered. Just be patient." *Easier said than done.* "Dallas seems to love your bed." Tired and dead on her feet, she wanted to sink onto that pillow top, dive under the heavy comforter and not move for three days. She'd go without food to just lie in one spot and not have to think about anything.

"You ready?"

She must have phased out leaning on the door frame because Jake stood in the hall holding a sofa cushion in one hand and pointing toward the bathroom with the other. "Aren't you going to shower?"

"Yep. And if you think I'm letting you wander the apartment…forget it." He pulled his handcuffs from his back pocket.

"Now, come on, Jake. Where do you think I can run dressed like this?"

"I turned my back on you twice and you disappeared on me. Twice. It's not happening again. Have a seat." He dropped the cushion in the doorway. She tried to pass and he took her left wrist gently, stroking the scratches she'd received while trying to free herself at the warehouse. "I wish I could keep it loose, Bree, but I'm afraid they don't work that way."

She knew and understood his dilemma. He rubbed a thumb across her pulse point, where the same handcuffs had rubbed her raw. The soothing circles of his fingers worked magic, but all too soon he put his arm around her and helped her sit. Then reaching behind her shoulders, his warm breath caressed her ear as he leaned to connect the second handcuff to the pipe under the sink.

The tickle made her tweak her neck close enough to the hero of the day she could kiss him. She wanted to. It would be the most natural thing in the world to lean just a bit forward…

Her eyes fluttered open as she caught her movement. Jake had met her halfway and their lips explored each other. Excitement mixed with longing and wonder, then an "oh, no, what am I doing" moment took over.

Their kiss was everything the connection she'd shared with him in the coffee shop had promised. And then some.

The sound of the handcuffs closing around the sink's drain caused her to pull back too far and bump her head on the wall. How embarrassing. She'd kissed him and he'd cuffed her.

"Ah…am I supposed to cover my eyes when you undress? Don't you feel a little awkward?" She wasn't clear if she spoke about the upcoming shower or the rising anticipation his touch had caused. She didn't close her eyes, keeping them completely open and noticing the day's growth of stubble on his jaw.

The lines etched into his face—were they from smiles or worries? His closeness made her curious to know which. His nearness mixed with a simple desire to want anything other than what was actually happening to her.

"Are you kidding?" He laughed. "I've been showering with other people for eight years. Six of those years were in a tent in the desert. Sharing a shower with one person is super easy."

He stood and unbuttoned the top button to his jeans as if she was another soldier. Her free hand smacked her eyes she covered them so quickly. She wanted to be casual about watching. If he weren't so darn cute or hadn't just kissed her and moved on like it was nothing, maybe it would be easier to watch him undress. She heard the loose jeans fall to the floor, the hamper lid as it dropped shut, the tub curtain pulled to the side and swished back into place. She was glad one of them didn't have a problem showering in front of others and wished she'd been brave enough to peek. She dropped her hand but kept her eyes shut, leaning her head against the hard wall.

Someone calling her name brought her back from the edge of a nightmare starring Larry in his black ski mask. His knife was about to cut more than her sweater.

"You were snoozing hard and fast there. Sorry to wake you, Sleeping Beauty, but can you toss me that towel on the sink? I can get it, but I'd be in my altogether."

Bree could see more through the opaque curtain than she'd imagined possible. The outline of his tall, lean body for one. She reached above her head for the towel and tossed it in his general direction. She'd seen his shoulders while he walked around bare chested. Well, not completely bare—it had the cutest amount of hair right where there should be.

"Thanks for taking such a quick shower." She gulped.

"No choice. All the hot water was gone." Behind the plain curtain, Jake shook the water from his hair, much like Dallas had earlier.

Bree admired his outline as he gingerly dabbed at the spot above his ear where he'd been shot. She was very grateful he wasn't asking her to answer questions. She was certain she'd forgotten how to speak.

Oh, my goodness. He stepped over the side of the tub with the towel splitting open across his thigh. Her eyes had to be popping from their sockets. She couldn't force them to close, her free hand refused to rise to her face and she was definitely no longer sleepy.

"I decided to save time and live with the stubble." He scratched his sexy jaw with his nails, creating a sound only stubble on a man's chin can make. She knew what his stubble against her cheek felt like, and darn it, she wanted to feel it there again.

Water droplets still clung to his tanned, hard chest. How could a man be so tan in the middle of winter? She wanted to know more about him. Why had he left the marine corps and how could he be so darn confident putting a plan into action to help her?

"I'll be back in a sec to unlock you."

There wasn't much space in the doorway. As tempting as he was to look at, she shifted and practically hugged the pipe with both arms. He passed behind her and she began to relax a little.

Then his towel shot over her head, landing in the tub. She dropped her face in her hands and heard roaring laughter behind her from his bedroom. He didn't shut the door.

Holy moly.

Chapter Thirteen

Bree expected the police or Larry and his cohort to pull up at any minute. In her opinion, they'd been at Jake's apartment too long. They had enough money to buy anything they needed and didn't need to waste time doing laundry.

But here she sat, nice and clean, full from a very good sandwich and cup of instant hot chocolate, waiting on her jeans and shoes to dry. An exhausted Dallas was curled on the couch cushion as her host gathered things for their trip.

Jake had finally let her call her family. She'd tried several times. No answer. Her heart pounded each time it rang, uncertain of what she'd say or how they'd take the news that she was alive.

Would they forgive her? Understand why she'd thought it was necessary to hide? And more than anything, were they okay or had Griffin's men already harmed them? The same questions she'd been asking herself while she'd been gone. She needed to get to Amarillo, find the answers and put an end to this story.

For the umpteenth time, she counted the cars in the parking lot and on as much of the street as she could see. The newest parked were easy to spot since another snow flurry had begun. There were two cars in the lot with snow melting on their warm hoods. But she was more curious about the tire tracks next to Jake's truck, where a car had come and gone.

Being mindful of her surroundings and if anyone followed her for any length of time was a way of life for her now. It hadn't prevented any of the events today, but she must have seen those men at some point. Where? They must have found her location and followed her around. Otherwise, how would they have known she was supposed to work for Brenda Ellen?

Sitting here, wearing only a robe, she was vulnerable and unprepared. But finally warm. Jake brought her an ancient handmade quilt as an extra layer before he joined Dallas on the couch.

Poor little Dallas. Even at six months old she slept a lot, but she needed to run and play. Maybe it would be better to leave her behind somewhere? It would be so hard to part with her, though.

Dallas had played in the warm shower like any Labrador who loved the water. Handing her over to Jake to be dried had been strangely intimate. She still wasn't certain which had been more embarrassing—him watching her throughout her shower or her watching him during his?

Actually, it hadn't been too intimidating undressing in front of him for some reason. She trusted that he'd kept his eyes shut. Trusting him was actually rather easy. Jake was the one who'd gotten soaked when Dallas shook the water from her fur. A lighthearted moment before he'd pulled off his shirt and tossed it in the hamper.

But she hadn't been laughing when he'd kissed her and handcuffed her to the pipes. Not only didn't he trust her to stay in the apartment, he didn't trust her to be cuffed to something comfortable in another room. And was totally avoiding any contact or repeat of their kiss.

"Does it make sense to just sit here? The longer we

wait, the harder it's going to be to get my family back. I can't call my uncle again until I get a replacement charger since you left mine in my suitcase." She took a deep breath before facing him, determined to stand her ground and move forward.

"You can't panic when we're delayed. Trust me. I made a couple of phone calls while you were in the shower. I'm not dragging my heels waiting on your clothes. I'm waiting on a marine buddy who's bringing some equipment.

"We should be on the road in a half hour or so. Anything about the weather?" he asked.

"Sorry, I had the sound down and was watching outside."

She tugged the belt of his terry-cloth robe tighter and hugged the collar closer to her neck. Under the robe she wore nothing. She'd chosen the hard footstool so she wouldn't fall asleep. She should be exhausted and terrified, but relaxing when she couldn't reach any of her family didn't make sense. She could only leave messages for her uncle, too.

Four paws in the air, Dallas stretched, laying her head on Jake's lap. Bree could easily be envious again. Of the soft cushions, not Jake's lap.

"When will your department notice the money's gone?" Bree asked as the clothes and tennis shoes tumbled dry in the background.

"They'll probably miss the phone Monday morning, but the money? No one found it before you called. You're lucky I hadn't been escorted from the building. A little earlier or later and I wouldn't have been able to help you."

"I feel terrible that you've lost your job. Do you think you can get it back?" She did feel bad. But if he hadn't been suspended, would he be helping her now? She had to count her blessings when she could.

"Maybe." He shrugged, the white of his undershirt out-lining his solid, broad shoulders. "Maybe I don't want it saved. I haven't decided. It's been an awkward promotion. I've known from day one it wasn't a great fit. They groomed another patrolman all last year. My military service fast-tracked me and, unfortunately, there was only one opening. It might have worked out in the long run, but it would have been a very long, lonely run to make. Enough about me, I need facts, Sabrina Watkins. You ready to tell me your story now?"

Had he just shared personal feelings with her? Was he trying to gain her confidence in spite of securing her to the bathroom floor? *Does it matter? You've got nowhere to go and no one to ask for help.*

"Do you know the guys who abducted you?" he asked. Leaning back, he stretched his neck from side to side before raising a water bottle and tossing two aspirin into his mouth.

"I can't identify them. They kept their masks on the entire time they had me in a car and an old warehouse. But I'd recognize the one called Larry. I don't think I'll forget his eyes. He had the same glare of the man who told Griffin I had to be killed. I'm praying he's not the one who has my family."

What was she going to do? She rose to wander the room, unable to be still. There weren't any boxes sitting in corners, but there were stacks of things that had been unpacked and just left.

"Now who's Griffin?" he asked. "You've mentioned him before."

"Is your friend ever going to get here?" She walked back to the balcony door, searching the lot again. Should she mention those tire tracks or ask him to let her in on his plan? *Trust works both ways, fella.*

"He's getting our supplies. Talk."

"Our families were friends in Silverton. Griffin Tyler is a bit older, got his veterinary license and started his own business in Amarillo. I owned a pet grooming and boarding business. Very small, but he asked me to join forces with him almost four years ago."

"So that's the business they took from you?"

She nodded. "They ended up setting fire to the building, after I stabbed Griffin with a scalpel."

"In self-defense?"

"He was trying to kill me."

He smiled. Even in the dim light from the hallway she could see the shine of his teeth. "What made you think they were trying to kill you?"

In spite of the conversation, Bree was very conscious she was undressed and couldn't leave. As much as she wanted to avoid discussing what happened on the day that changed her life, she couldn't steal his keys that he'd left near the door and just go. He'd catch her as she fought to keep the robe together while running down the sidewalk.

"The gun for starters. I know a lot of long-haul truckers, my dad's friends," she continued. "I'd groom their dogs when they stopped in Amarillo. I usually worked two Sundays a month. That day, I finished early and decided to check on the animals we were boarding for the weekend. My assistant had gone to a wedding or baby shower and couldn't get by until much later. That's when I overheard them talking. The evil guy—his eyes gleamed when he spoke about killing—he was there telling Griffin what their orders were."

"And you saw his face?"

She shivered when the image of the man popped into her mind. "I can't forget what he looked like. The nightmares keep it fresh. I've never remembered things so vividly before. There was just something evil about the way he looked when he mentioned killing. I hate the nightmares."

Jake looked as though he sympathized and understood. Did he have nightmares from his experience in the military?

"So you…" He urged her to finish while stroking Dallas gently between the ears.

She searched the titles of books stacked in the corner instead of Jake's face. She shouldn't wonder about his dreams or what his life was like. She had too much to think about as things stood. "I knew I needed to get out of there fast. I ran for my van, hoping they hadn't seen me. Then I remembered the animals. If they were going to 'torch' the place, like they'd discussed, all the animals I was boarding would die. I couldn't let that happen."

"Just like you couldn't let Dallas stay at the shelter and risk no one adopting her?"

"It took three months to talk Brenda Ellen into taking her home and if I wasn't there, they might have…" She didn't want to think about the animals she hadn't gotten homes for—there'd always be too many. "Why did you think I'd come back for her?"

"Don't know. An impression from the connection you two seem to have with each other." His voice was low, like he almost didn't want to admit that she could care. "So where did the money come from?"

More reality. She hadn't shared the details of that night with anyone, but they were as clear as ever. She'd written them down so she wouldn't forget. Everything was in her electronic journal that she hoped would be impossible for anyone to find.

"Griffin must have heard me moving pet carriers. He caught me just after I loaded the last cat and forced me back to his office. We fought. I grabbed an open briefcase.

I escaped in my grooming van, leaving it in front of another animal clinic."

"Why not go to the police and explain what you overheard? You could identify the guy and they could have protected you." His east Texas twang became more prominent.

Just like when he'd been irritated with her earlier. Which part had upset him? Not going to the police? Or not identifying a potential killer?

"I overheard Griffin say that someone in the police department would help with the cover-up. The evil guy wasn't too pleased with a cop's involvement but said it would help when they blamed me. I was so confused. I drove around in the van with three dogs and a kitten, too scared to talk with anyone. I just kept driving around in circles."

It was doubtful a confident marine would ever feel as scared as she had been that night. She could see the framed commendations stacked on a bookshelf instead of hanging on the wall. Maybe she'd ask her own questions about his past one day. But right now, they had to concentrate on putting Griffin and his cohorts in jail.

"The fire was huge and could be seen for miles. Griffin made a statement for the radio claiming he'd confronted me about embezzling and that the police were searching for me. The next day, I was…my remains were positively identified in the fire. That meant they'd not only switched the dental records but had killed a woman. It sort of confirmed they had someone on the police force. I didn't know who to trust."

"I'd think the same thing. It's amazing that you managed to stay under the radar so long. How did you get from Amarillo to Dallas? And how in the world did you end up as a dog sitter?" He smiled and sort of laughed at the last words.

"You wouldn't know this, but I started my business

by pet sitting and dog walking. Some of us didn't have money for college or fancy careers and made the best of very difficult times."

He rose from the couch, carefully moving Dallas's head as he got up. In a heartbeat he stood in front of her and tilted her chin to look at him. "I didn't mean to insult you. We just met this morning, but I can tell how much you love animals. It's a good fit."

She had been momentarily hurt. Right up until she looked into his concerned eyes. *Remember that you're alone and vulnerable. You have to stay strong.* She had an uneasy feeling and searched the parking lot. Snowflakes fell, melting as they hit the warmer blacktop or refreshing the piles of snow from the previous two days.

"There was more than money in the briefcase. A list of names I've been checking. All of them have pets and lived around Lakewood. I thought I heard the evil guy say the higher-ups were in this area, but I haven't found any connection. All I accomplished was getting Brenda Ellen killed and you suspended."

"Don't do that to yourself. Nothing good will come from it. There's no retreat and no going back." Jake stared somewhere over her head.

At first she thought he'd stopped speaking because he'd seen something. But she quickly realized he spoke from experience and had changed his mind about explaining.

"Let me think a little while about what you've told me," he said finally. "We can talk more in the truck."

"Is there an all-night store nearby? We need dog food for Dallas. She needs something more suited for her than lunch meat." She joined the puppy on the couch, needing her unconditional comfort. The dryer buzzed.

"It's been taken care of." He followed her to the couch

and stroked Dallas on the crown of her head. "You know, we can ask my pal to take care of her."

Strong, lean, long fingers…so close to her breasts and a robe she felt compelled to flatten across them was all she could focus on. If the circumstances had been different… She shook her head, answering his question about Dallas and saying no to her attraction. Jake's extra care with her pet touched her deeply. "I'm probably being selfish, but I'd like to keep her with me. She's been through so much, I don't know how she'll react if I leave her behind."

"Got it."

Maybe he considered the Lab his now? If it was his intention to send her to jail, she couldn't keep a puppy. Either way, he treated Dallas in a loving manner. And unfortunately for Bree, it was very attractive. She had to remember that Jake Craig intended to put her in jail and she couldn't let him succeed.

Jake answered his house phone by just listening. No words, then he set it back on the charger. "Can you two go to the bedroom for a minute? Mac's here." He withdrew his gun from the holster and stood at the door, ready for the worst. "We've got what we need now and will be leaving in five."

Bree kept the bedroom door cracked a fraction, trying to listen after Jake let his friend into the apartment. They spoke too low. She couldn't get a glimpse of what the other marine looked like, just the large black bag Jake set on the floor and the five or six bills that he counted into the other man's extended hand.

The puppy whined. "Shh, girl, we'll be okay."

We have to be.

She didn't know Jake well and he'd just admitted that he probably wasn't returning to law enforcement. Could she really trust that he wasn't after the money?

Whatever his motives, she had to take advantage of his help to free her family and waltz around the hot attraction that sizzled with each look.

Chapter Fourteen

Jake berated himself for not checking the weather before leaving Dallas. Once they'd gotten north of Fort Worth, it had begun snowing hard. He hadn't thought too much about a snow flurry at the apartment. He'd driven through them before. No big deal. They had food and a full tank of gas.

Two hours north and he was barely moving twenty miles per hour down the highway. They followed the few drivers brave enough or foolish enough to keep pushing forward. But now even those cars were exiting to a closed gas station.

"Need some coffee?" Bree stretched awake from the sound sleep she'd needed. "Oh, they don't look open."

"Afraid we're stuck here awhile."

"But we can't stop. We don't have time."

"I can't see the road any longer. Not to mention the ice already on the bridges." He was physically tired of driving through the crosswinds hitting the truck. And when he was this exhausted, he could lose control. He wouldn't let that happen. He knew how to avoid that dark place.

"But—"

"Look, I want you to get there ASAP. I don't feel comfortable helping you escape from the Dallas P.D., but I realize this is the best solution for you, me and your family. I also want us to get there alive. Everyone's pulled off of 287." He slipped his gloves on, immediately regretting the harshness he'd used to speak to her. "I'm going to check with the truck driver we were following. See if he received word about road conditions or if he was just tired of fighting this wind."

He pulled the keys. Dallas popped her head up when the cab light came on. "Stay."

"Do you really think we'd try to go anywhere?" Bree asked.

"I was talking to Dallas."

"Right. Want to cuff me again?"

He closed the door without letting the wind slam it shut. It was tense enough in the truck just driving. He didn't need the wrath of a woman to aggravate the situation. The snow didn't fall as much as it slammed against his exposed skin. He quickly zipped his jacket and pulled the collar up around his neck.

"This dang wind makes this morning's walk in the snow feel warm."

In the military police, he hadn't been in the middle of many blizzards and sure hadn't faced them in east Texas, where he'd grown up. That gut-wrenching instinct told him this wasn't a normal snowstorm. He had a very bad feeling they'd be stuck until morning. If not here, then along the road away from any town or cell reception.

The wind gusted enough to blow him sideways as he walked. He wasn't a lightweight and had to shield his face with his hand to see the vehicles in front of him. The tire tracks of the car that they had pulled off with were almost gone. As he passed, he noticed the man inside was alone and bundled into a sleeping bag in the backseat.

Jake jogged as best as he could to the big rig and tapped on the door. The driver gestured through the closed window for him to go around to the other side. When he got there, the door was cracked open and he climbed up. He was greeted by a very large man holding a wooden bat.

"A. B. Mills. You need something?"

"Jake Cra—Crain." He caught himself before using his real name. "I was wondering if you had news of road conditions into Amarillo?"

"Slow going and icy bridges to Wichita Falls. Not much movement west on I-40 right now. No rescue vehicles can get through the storm. Everyone's hunkered down and there's talk they'll close the highway. You might have better luck waiting it out till morning. That's my plan."

"That's what I thought."

"You in the car or the truck?" A. B. Mills never put the bat down. He just kept tapping or twisting it in his palm, sending a very loud message not to mess with him.

"Truck. Guy in the car's already camping there."

"In a hurry to make Amarillo?"

"As a matter of fact, yeah. Family emergency."

"Your truck got four-wheel drive? If so, get you some weight in the back end and you won't slide around as much. Slow and steady. You might hit I-40 in five or so hours."

"Thanks. I better get back and let my…wife know."

"Just pick you up a couple of logs or something like that. Good luck."

"Thanks again." Jake braced himself for the blast of cold.

He and Bree weren't completely unprepared to stay on the side of the road. They had coats and gloves. But the only blanket belonged to the dog. There was no extra gas if they stayed put and ran the truck's heater to stay warm. Being one swing away from striking out was wearing a bit on his nerves.

He'd come up with a plan, got MacMahan to bring him every piece of electronics he could think of…but hadn't followed through each time he'd begun to check the friggin' weather.

Walking between vehicles was so cold, the truck seemed like a hothouse to him by the time he sat inside. Dallas was curled in a tight ball and his prisoner shivered. He quickly started the engine and put the heater on high.

"Sorry about that. I should have left the truck running."

"I don't blame you. If you'd left the keys, you might be hitching a ride with one of the other drivers."

"Is that a warning that you need to be handcuffed to the steering wheel from now on?"

"Not hardly. As much as I want to do this on my own, I know I can't. Did the trucker know anything?"

He repeated the information he'd received and Bree visibly reacted the way he felt. "We can't wait here all night. Jerry's usually in Amarillo every Sunday. We'll miss him if we're not there. He's a trucker. He leaves tomorrow night."

"Whoa, wait a minute. Who's Jerry and why do we need to meet up with him? The plan's to collect the money from your uncle."

"Uncle Jerry hid the money. That's why I needed the phone. He's the only person who knows I'm still alive."

"You gave a truck driver almost two million dollars to hide? Man alive." He threw his cap and gloves onto the backseat. "You really think he's just going to hand it back over?"

"He's my mom's brother." She rubbed her hands together in front of the heater vent. "He kept the money safe."

Should he explain human nature to her and how unlikely a prospect it was that this man still had the money? "Is there a particular reason you waited until now to tell me?"

"Maybe because of the way you're reacting. Are we staying here or driving?"

"Going. But it won't be fun."

"As if any of today has been?"

"You have a point." He understood her sarcasm better than anyone else who'd been a part of their day. He slammed the truck into Drive. The spinning tires emphasized more than just his frustration. "The ice is going to be a problem."

"Would you like me to drive? I was raised here in the Panhandle. I'm used to it."

He shot her a look like she might be crazy. She wasn't watching him, just the road. She was serious. Maybe she wouldn't attempt an escape. That didn't mean he'd let his guard down. This woman had a habit of slipping away from him when he turned his back. Or worse, she'd slipped under his radar and broken his personal perimeter.

"I'll tough it out. Is there anything else I should know before we get to Amarillo?" Jake's foot itched to go faster, but twenty to thirty miles per hour was all the truck could manage without sliding across both lanes.

"I'm not sure." Bree clicked the radio to AM and pushed the scan button. It landed on excited, rapid talking. Spanish news.

He didn't speak Spanish and opened his mouth to tell her, but she shushed him, turning the faint station irritatingly louder. Dallas perked up, paws on the seat. Bree coaxed her over the top and had her head quickly dropping onto her lap.

Bree turned the radio off and leaned back. She was deep in thought somewhere and wasn't eager to share what she'd deciphered.

"Did you understand any of that?" he asked.

"I can pick out the major words and assume enough to fill in the blanks."

Patience wasn't his virtue, but he waited. Both hands

on the wheel to keep the wind from blowing the truck into the ditch. There hadn't been any lights in the past mile. Visibility was down to almost nothing. No headlights. No taillights. No points of light indicating a small town.

"What's the verdict?"

"As best as I can understand, there's a whiteout in Amarillo. All the traffic's been diverted off Interstate 40 and they're warning people to get to safety."

The rear of the truck slid back and forth for several seconds as they passed over another iced bridge. "Maybe that's what we should do."

Bree seemed to handle sliding across the highway well. She gripped Dallas with one arm and the safety handle with her other. If she was panicky, there wasn't any outward sign.

"We can't turn back. Please. We have to keep trying or they'll—"

"Kill your family. I know. But if we're in an accident, there's even less chance of helping them. Our best shot is to call the local cops and get your family to safety."

"You know that won't work."

"I know you *think* these men—whoever they are—have someone on the payroll, but every cop in Amarillo can't be. The odds of something like that happening—"

He saw the fright in her eyes and released his right hand to cover hers. A second, maybe two, and they were careening onto the grassy median. Black ice under the fresh snow or another gust of wind sent them onto the icier shoulder and began the spin.

Jake pumped the breaks and steered into the turn, but it didn't help. They were out of control and could only pray nothing like a ditch, concrete barrier or parked car got in their way.

"Brace yourself."

BREE HAD BARELY wrapped an arm around Dallas to hold her steady before latching onto the shoulder strap. The truck spun and she closed her eyes, unwilling to watch their out-of-control fate. The sickening feeling lessened as the truck slowed to a stop and she realized they'd come out unscathed.

They hadn't hit anything, hadn't rolled over and were barely in a ditch. Jake released the steering wheel, put it in Park, rubbed his neck and extended his arms to the ceiling as if he was on a long-overdue break.

"You and Dallas okay?" he asked while stretching his neck from side to side.

"I think so." The pup was shaking but stayed in her lap. "My heart thinks it's still spinning in circles, though."

Jake's laugh was full of tension but warmed her.

"We're turning back and that's the last word. It's too dangerous, Bree."

He sounded final and she couldn't think of a thing to change his mind. The only thoughts filling her brain were of those maddening, murderous eyes and what they'd do to her family.

The truck inched forward, Jake slowly gave it gas and, miraculously, they weren't stuck. If it were possible to go slower than he'd already been driving, he did. The snow obscured everything in front of them and she had no idea how Jake could see well enough to keep on the road.

"We'll return to the parking lot and call or use the trucker's CB for assistance. Worst-case scenario is we wait until the peak of the storm passes."

"Maybe the storm's not as bad west of here. We could go back to Decatur and try west to Lubbock, then north to Amarillo?"

Jake released a long sigh filled with the frustration she felt down to her frozen toes.

The shrill ring of an old-fashioned telephone had her and Dallas jumping in their seats. She seemed to be sitting on the receiver, but it wasn't possible. Both phones were on the dashboard, where he'd tossed them after talking to the trucker.

"How did you get a cell past me?" he accused. "Hand it over. Now."

"I didn't and I don't have one. It has to be them. They're watching us, just like they said, and they know we've turned around."

"That's impossible. There's not another car around for miles. Nothing's moving on these roads."

He guided the truck to the shoulder of the highway and cut the engine. She set Dallas back in her dog bed between them, unbelted and had to dig through several items under the seat. It was hard to see, but the phone lit up when it rang.

"Here it is."

"Got it." He took the cell from her extended hand. "Look, Bree. Whatever I say to them, remember I'm on your side. I give you my word. If they can call us, that means we can call the authorities to get your family protection."

His fingertips and palm absorbed her racing pulse without calming her in the least. She knew the voice on the other end of that ring. And also knew that Jake couldn't keep that promise no matter how much he tried.

Griffin's men already had her family or they would have answered their phones. Three cells and a house phone wouldn't all be out because of the blizzard. She knew they had been abducted.

"This is Craig," he answered on speaker.

"You go back, her family dies." The voice from her

nightmares coldly commanded. "The phone stays with you or her family dies. We'll stay in touch."

He disconnected.

The screen lit again and Jake mumbled some words she'd like to shout in the face of the man who haunted her.

"What is it?" she asked. Fearful tears blurred her vision and prevented her focusing when he flipped the phone around for her to see.

"I assume this is your family?"

She wiped her eyes, wanting to stay hidden behind her palms, but she had to answer. The small image took shape. She nodded, recognizing the small porch leading up to the old front door that her mother painted red at the beginning of each new year. Red for prosperity and good fortune.

But in front of the door, her family were on their knees in the snow. Hands zip-tied, no coats or winter protection and completely helpless with three guns pointing at their heads.

"The snow is barely covering the ground. The radio said it's been snowing hard since three this afternoon. When Griffin found out I didn't have the money...he said he'd do this."

Jake touched the screen of the cell. "Dammit, password protected. I can't call them or turn the GPS off." He flipped the phone to remove the cover.

"Please don't. They need to know exactly where we're at. We should get moving. Now."

"I still think we should call the Amarillo P.D."

"Detective Craig, what made you decide to help me? Not very long ago you said you didn't know if you wanted your job back or not. So why are you helping me?"

He tapped the steering wheel with his long index fingers, either trying to create a reason or carefully planning his words. She knew exactly why she'd stayed with Jake.

Her choices were limited. She either accepted his help or went to jail. His reasons weren't that clear-cut. At least not to her.

"Is it that tough a question?" she prodded.

"I want to be honest," he said.

"With me or yourself?"

He made a grunting *hmm* sound and continued his search out the windows. "Do you need my jacket?"

"No, just your answer." She recognized the confused, questioning, furrowed brow. Too many people looked at her the same way. As if she were foolish to want her own business instead of attending college. And then again when she went into partnership with Griffin. "I'm not crazy and I have a logical reason for asking. I want to know your motivation."

"Not following. Who said you were crazy?"

"You see, Detective—"

"Jake."

"No, right now, you're being the police detective who feels obligated to get help from his brothers in arms. Thing is, *Detective,* you've already ruled out that would work, or you would have turned me over to the Dallas P.D. So can we stop going over the same failed idea and come up with a plan that might actually have some merit?"

Even masking his words by his hand and mumbling in a low growl didn't keep her from deciphering the expletives probably common to a marine.

"My gut's normally right. I make a decision, then I run with it. No second-guessing myself." He scratched his chin, then the top of his head, acting a little confused. "I made up my mind while leaving my captain's office I would help you. A few minutes before you asked."

"So we're agreed that the police aren't the wisest course of action?"

"As much as I hate to admit it, yes. You're stuck with me."

"Thanks, Jake. So if we're not returning…"

"Got it." He cranked the engine and eased back onto the highway.

During their time in the median, not one car had passed. There wasn't a light within sight. The weather situation was probably worse than what Jake feared. But there weren't any alternative solutions.

"I wasn't kidding about driving," she said, calmer than she felt. "This isn't my first blizzard and I've driven lots of trucks."

"I've spent a few days in a bad climate or two. Harsh weather. Drastic temperatures. Wind blowing sand so hard you felt like each pellet was piercing your skin." Jake eased the truck across the highway. Slow and steady toward the exit.

His voice had grown harder, far away, sad. She didn't mean to make him relive his battles in the Middle East.

"You can count on me until we get everything straightened out. No more questioning where our loyalties lie. Your family's in danger and we'll work together." He didn't hesitate or argue that the overpass was too dangerous. He edged the truck forward, maintaining control, and got them headed north again.

"Thank you, Jake."

"These bastards plan to kill all of us. You know that, right?"

"Yes." She could barely say the word.

"You're right about the police. Going to them isn't an option. But once we get the money, we'll be in charge. We need a better plan."

Chapter Fifteen

"That one! That's his rig." Bree shouted, unfastening her seat belt and preparing to jump from the truck. "Just pull up behind him and we can knock on the door."

It hadn't been that long since Jake had knocked on A. B. Mills's door. He remembered the baseball bat clear as a bell. "Hold on. Let's make sure no one's watching him. Or us."

"But no one knows about Jerry."

"You didn't think anyone knew you were working for Richardson, either. Let's take this one step at a time. You told him you'd call. We'll gas up and see if anyone pulls in acting suspicious."

Jerry Riley's rig hadn't been there too long. Where the other trucks they passed were covered in snow, his looked like it had parked recently. He was also parked across the street. They'd searched two truck stops for her uncle and each time they'd called he hadn't answered. But he'd warned them that might be the case. Spotty cell coverage and the basic fact that he needed both hands on the wheel fighting the dangerous fifty-mile-per-hour wind gusts.

Before Jerry answered his phone, he'd been at a rest area, safe from those winds that could turn a truck his size over. After learning their family was in danger, he agreed to fight the winds and meet them in Wichita Falls.

With the parking lot full to the brim, Jake drove to the pumps, amazed that dozens of trucks had enough room for their doors to open and nothing more. No space between their engines and the back of the next trailer.

Jake filled up and Bree stood next to him dialing. "No answer."

"You folks look tired. Come a long way?" A squeaky voice said behind him.

The roar of the wind and loud flapping of the metal canopy must have hidden the approach of the young man. Jake was momentarily taken back to a sandstorm in the Afghanistan desert, searching for his enemy. He shook it off, but his hand had already landed on his weapon.

The bright orange jumpsuit with the gas logo emblazoned front and back indicated a legitimate attendant. At least for the time being. "I can take care of this if you folks want to wait inside. It's not a problem."

"No, thanks. Where can we park when we're done?" he asked, still watching for cars or men watching him. The visibility was just too low to see anything moving more than thirty feet away—nothing was clearly defined.

"Well, if you're staying for the duration, we've got a row going in the back. There's room for four or five more cars end to end. All the motels are booked up. They was the first to go last night when we got word they was shutting down the highway."

Being blocked in would never work. Bree looked anxious that he would even consider staying here, pinned down in the car jungle. "We just need a short break. The wind's fairly bad."

"You know the highway's shut down from here past Amarillo. Highway patrol won't let anything past 'em." The attendant removed the pump and stowed it.

"We're not driving too far," he lied, and saw the confusion on the kid's face. "We were running on fumes and thought we should fill up. Patty here just had to make sure her mother was home safe yesterday, but I couldn't stay there another minute."

"Gotcha." The attendant pointed to the street just north of Jerry's rig. "If you ain't staying, I gotta ask that you park off the premises. We're keeping things as orderly as possible, but the lot's not good for anyone who wants to leave before they give the all clear."

"We completely understand. Any idea how long they think the storm's lasting?" Bree asked. "Um…my mom's satellite was out and we weren't getting reception on these." She held up the phone he'd stolen from the police.

"Could be the rest of today. Amarillo had over a foot of snow drop on her overnight. Sun might help, but we have to wait on the bridges and drifts to be cleared. Storm's headed northeast, but they're still not advising travel south of us yet. If that's everything, I'm going back inside to some warmth." The kid waved his gloves and disappeared on the other side of the truck.

Dallas howled at the kid as he disappeared around the corner. Jake took a long time staring toward the highway, hearing nothing except the loose canopy that might fly free at any minute. If someone was out there watching, he'd never know.

"No luck getting your uncle?"

They moved the truck closer to Jerry's. Bree shook the cell and dropped it on the seat. "It's a cheap little prepaid phone from a truck stop just like this place. He's probably asleep in his rig."

Jake parked, careful to leave enough room in front of his truck in case they needed to leave in a hurry. "You stay here with the doors locked."

"But—"

"But nothing. We limit our risks. There was one thing we both agreed on earlier. I'm giving the orders." He killed the engine, snatched the keys and jumped out, avoiding further discussion.

"I don't think I really agreed to anything," she said as the door closed.

The wind slammed him into his fender before he crossed the street. The closer they'd driven to Wichita Falls, the more local weather reports they'd picked up on the radio. The wind was gusting somewhere between fifty-five and seventy miles per hour and yet the storm was creeping through the area. He believed it. Visibility was down to almost zero.

Traveling to Amarillo right now was a stupid idea, but he knew Bree would steal his truck or steal another, taking back roads around the barricades before waiting or giving up. He went to the passenger side of the rig and climbed on the rail, but before he could catch a glimpse inside a quick yank had him falling on his butt in the drift.

When he looked up, a giant of a man stood steady in the whirling snow. "Hey, boy. This is your third look at my rig. What do you want?"

"Are you Jerry Riley?"

"You Craig?"

The answering grin confirmed he was Bree's uncle. When Jake responded with a firm nod, the giant grabbed his gloved hands, pulled him to his feet and pumped his arms until he thought they might come loose from their sockets.

"I was beginning to worry. Where's my girl? Is she all right? I heard the phone but couldn't answer it in these high winds while driving and then had to get some grub. I can't wait to see her and make sure she's okay. Have you told her parents she's alive yet?"

Jake didn't crane his neck to look up at very many people, but he did tilt his head back to look Bree's uncle Jerry in the eye. The wind was so bad they both had to raise their voices to be heard. Someone could be standing ten feet away and listen to parts of their conversation without being seen.

"I'd like to keep this as low-key as possible, sir. I'm not sure you should see her right—"

"Uncle Jerry!" Bree bounded into Jerry's arms. He lifted her off the ground without the wind or snow bothering him at all. The man planted his feet and wasn't budging.

"Oorah. Good to see you, little lady."

Jerry Riley wasn't just built like a marine, he *was* a retired marine. *Oorah.* Jake let them have a private moment, taking advantage to search the perimeter he could see. Maybe he shouldn't allow a conversation that he couldn't hear, but he couldn't have prevented it. He kept his hand on his weapon, expecting to be charged or fired upon at any minute.

If he had been the person tracking them, he'd verify what just transpired before an attack. But why would they assume the money wasn't in Amarillo as she'd said? The phone Larry had left in his truck to track them—or the GPS phone as they'd begun calling it—was still in the front seat. There was no telling what would happen once Larry and his sidekick noticed they were in Wichita Falls for an extended period. One thing he'd had drilled into him since entering the corps, you could never predict when your opponents would strike.

"Let's get moving," Jerry said. "These old bones don't like the cold too much. So you do what you gotta do and I'll be ready to go in fifteen. Just need to move my rig into the lot."

"Wait." Big man or not, Jake pulled him to a stop by grabbing his arm. "We just need the package."

"Jerry can help," Bree said.

"We agreed," he spoke to her, "that he'd take the GPS phone to Amarillo when the roads open. We advance from the south highway and get to Amarillo without them knowing. We take them by surprise and keep the leverage. It's the best plan." He turned to Jerry, whose face was a blank slate. "I appreciate the offer to help, but you know I'm right."

"Sabrina, darlin', can you check on Charlie for me? He refuses to do his business in the cold."

"But—"

Uncle Jerry's suggestion didn't receive as much debate as Jake's did when she disagreed with a decision. One look at his niece and she performed an about-face and climbed into the warm truck. He caught a glimpse of that perfect backside encased in tight jeans and...yeah, he could do with some heating up himself.

The door clicked shut and before Jake could fully focus on Jerry, a fist connected with his jaw. The second time alone with this marine and Jake was making snow angels on the side of the road.

He moved his jaw back and forth to verify it still worked, and paused, debating where to hit this man to bring him down. Then Jerry extended his hand to help him back to his feet.

"I could ask what that was for, but I think I know." If he'd caught someone looking at his niece the way he'd just looked at Bree, they wouldn't be standing, either.

"And I'm betting you don't know why. It was to make a point I haven't stated yet."

"Okay, I'm biting." And wanting out of the blizzard that

was knocking them both into the side panel of his trailer. "Am I just tired or is the wind blowing harder?"

"I know Sabrina wants to get the money and take off. But I just caught you unawares because you're not just tired, you're exhausted. So, you either take me with you and I do the driving around those barricades. Or you stay here until the bulk of the storm passes, 'cause that ain't your imagination about the wind."

"I can't take you with me, Jerry. And unfortunately—" he rubbed his sore jaw "—there's no way she's going to stay put."

"I thought you'd say that. And, yes, I know my niece. The same young woman who's been hiding for six months instead of endangering her family. They've reported seventy-five-mile-per-hour winds blowing snow and small vehicles across the road. There's no physical way to get to our family without encountering this storm. None. And for who you're going to face, you'll need all your strength when you arrive. I guarantee that driving in hurricane-force winds isn't just tiring, it's downright stupid."

"What do you suggest? They're tracking us via a GPS in a cell. When it doesn't move, the guys following us are going to come looking for it."

"Let 'em find it. Give me the keys to your truck, climb on up in my sleeper with Sabrina and hand me that pug, Charlie."

Jake pulled the keys from his pocket. "I should go get Dallas."

"If Dallas is a dog—and knowing that niece of mine, it is—I'll take care of it. Lock the doors and get some sleep."

"First, I need to flush out some wolves."

Jerry rubbed his gloves together. "I've been ready for a good hunt for six months."

Chapter Sixteen

The wind whistled down the chimney flue, pushing a small puff of smoke into Griffin Tyler's living room. As many times as he'd hired professionals to fix the problem, his eyes still watered when he lit a fire. He tossed another log into the opening to build up the flame and warm the room. The bourbon no longer helped as he sent the last shot down his gullet.

Five years of "favors" were beginning to take their toll on him. And now those idiots had killed another woman. They should have killed the right woman in the first place, then life would be easier.

"I hate that bitch!"

No one heard him scream his frustration. He needed to be free from owing "favors." But that should be soon. Constantly working or creating ways to launder the larger and larger amounts of money showing up each week was wearing thin.

The second phone he'd nicknamed his "favor" line vibrated on the bar behind him.

At first money laundering had been an easy way to pay off a gambling debt. Not too difficult to list fictitious surgeries. Animals would come in, he'd write up the bill and he'd be paid in cash. Several grand a week he could handle. Larger amounts of money caused problems when Sabrina began asking questions about unnecessary boardings or animals that weren't there. She was gone and he had a new clinic that cost much less than the books showed, and here he was again on the verge of losing everything.

"I really do hate that troublesome bitch."

If Sabrina hadn't stolen his briefcase, he would have disappeared six months ago. He should be somewhere tropical, free of the money-laundering operation and this stress. Free of the threats from murderers and men who would never let him stop. He might escape if he got to the two million before his silent "partner" and if he could disappear during a blizzard.

The phone rattled on the granite countertop again. The wind shook the windows. Three in the morning and it hadn't eased up for twelve hours. He'd have to get the roofer to verify the shingles were still attached.

He dreaded answering. There could only be two people on the other end of the call—Leroy or Leroy's brother, Larry. Those weren't their real names, but he hadn't cared to learn the real ones. Larry and another no-name lowlife were following Sabrina and her cop. He didn't want to hear from them until they found the money, but the damn blizzard was screwing with everything. In particular, the deadline to return the money.

"Hard to believe this started with a string of bad bets on a few football games." He stood from the lounge chair and poured himself the remaining bourbon. The phone vibrated again.

Nothing in Amarillo was moving—not even the police. He could only assume that Larry was reporting that they'd stopped, too. He'd have to answer the blasted thing.

"Yes?"

"Something's up, man. They're in Wichita Falls talking to some old fart. We can't get close enough to hear," Larry whispered into the phone.

"What do you think I can do about it?"

"The boss said I should check in with you and you'd handle it. That's what I'm doing. I can take my orders from him, but I'm thinkin' that's not exactly what you want me to do."

Griffin understood the threat. Any problem and the hired muscle would eliminate him right along with Sabrina and her new boyfriend.

"Where are they?"

"Same place as every other car that could make it this far, man, a truck stop."

That's why it was difficult to hear Larry speak. The background voices and distorted music coming from overhead speakers nearly drowned out Larry's voice.

"Does the man have a dog? She could know him from her pet grooming business. Or they could be asking a stranger about the freakin' whiteout between there and Amarillo. Are they still talking to him?"

"It looks like they're headed inside and the old guy's heading to his big rig. Hold on—"

Griffin put the call on speaker and leaned on the bar, waiting. He'd stayed awake specifically to handle this mess.

"The old man's looking through stuff."

"Stay with them and keep back. Call me when they start moving again. If anyone gives them anything, make sure it's the money before you move in. I don't care what it takes, you have that money back here in twenty-four hours."

"Do you still want the woman brought to you?" he asked.

"No, let's let the police take care of the problem you

created yesterday. Let her take the fall for the woman you killed. That's only if you aren't forced to kill her alongside her new boyfriend. I really don't care. Just get me the money."

He clicked the phone off and tipped the rest of the bourbon down his throat, hearing the fire pop behind him. He could finally get some sleep. He set the tumbler in the bar sink, feeling the past six months of stress lifting from his shoulders. It was nearly over.

"Hello, Griffin."

The maniacal voice came from the dark near the kitchen.

"Leroy?" He was early. Most likely preventative insurance to make certain the money got back into their hands. "I wasn't expecting you until Monday."

He shrugged. "We ran into a situation that needed your input." He crossed to the back door and shoved it open.

Three people stood in at least two feet of snow that had blown onto his porch. They were bound and gagged and he recognized them immediately. Sabrina's family.

"They can't be here. Are you crazy?"

"Some people have said so." He yanked Darlene through the threshold and her parents followed.

Half frozen, pure hatred burned into him from the glares of the bitch's parents. Confusion and tears from her sister. Griffin didn't care. There was no reason to offer them comfort or feel pity for them. Now that they knew of his involvement, they'd have to be killed as soon as Larry arrived with the money.

Watkins should have shot these men before allowing them to take his wife and daughter. The man holding a gun on Sabrina's family didn't come inside. He scurried away like the scorpion he was, hiding in the dark until he could prey on his victims.

"What's the problem?"

"The boss is closing down this branch of operations." Leroy's heavy-lidded eyes were dark slits in his squinty face.

No more favors? "When?"

"I thought that would make you happy," he mocked. "You'll know when soon enough. You got a place to keep these three awhile? A secure room? Maybe a cellar?"

"I have a storm shelter out back. Once it's locked, there's no getting in or out. The key's by the back door."

Watkins made a muffled protest or something. His wife's tears continued to fall. The two of them knew they were going to die and had no idea why any of this was happening. Just like they had no idea Sabrina was still alive. It helped having friends in the Amarillo P.D., who switched the dental records.

Leroy whistled and his apprentice scurried back through the door. "Put these three in the storm thing in the backyard. Key's by the door."

The three were shoved through his kitchen at gunpoint. He caught himself opening his mouth to protest, but he couldn't show that he cared. And he didn't. Not for the reasons someone might think.

The only reason he'd protest is that the Watkins family would probably be shot in his storm cellar and be left to rot there. If he got the money before Leroy, he would be out of here so fast.

"Larry called. Did he get the money?" Leroy asked, sitting on the arm of the lounger.

"He thought Sabrina would have it soon. Once he gets it, he'll call again."

"Right."

The fire crackled and popped in the background, and the wind still shook the windows during its bigger gusts.

He was at a loss. What kind of a conversation was he supposed to have with a hit man for gamblers? He stood there like an idiot. He hadn't had too much contact with Leroy since the fire and still didn't know the true identity of the woman who died instead of Sabrina. He didn't want to know. The less he knew about the operation, the better.

He'd do his favors until they shut him down or until he could skip town with the money. Whichever situation presented itself, he'd take advantage. He always had.

"Want a drink or something?"

"Do you have a beer?" Leroy asked, standing and following him to the bar.

Griffin moved to the small fridge behind the counter and grabbed an import. "So how long do you think until they're through with me?"

He stood and was met in the face with a gun barrel.

Leroy shrugged. "Now?"

The urge to run was great, but for some reason he couldn't move. The bottle dropped, shattering at his feet. Leroy threw back his head, laughing. He focused on the finger squeezing the trigger and—

Chapter Seventeen

"You're really okay waiting here?" Jake asked one last time.

"Jerry's a professional driver. If he says he can't drive your truck to Amarillo, then we're forced to wait. I'm not thrilled about staying in the sleeper of his rig, but I admit that neither of us has slept in two days. He made a good point about how ineffective we'd be rescuing my family. It's hard to argue with him, but that doesn't make the worrying go away."

Jake had compromised with Jerry. Logic told him that the guys in Dallas were following. He wanted a chance to flush them out, to see if Larry or Griffin Tyler would call, asking why they were delayed in Wichita Falls. The GPS phone was in his pocket and they were inside the convenience store where the signal was stronger.

"Ten more minutes and we're hitting the hay." So far the phone hadn't rung and he hadn't spotted anyone interested in them. But he couldn't shake the feeling that someone had eyes on his back. "I admit your uncle isn't exactly like I imagined."

"What did you expect? Some grumpy old fat man who drove a truck?" She laughed exactly like she had at the diner the day before. "I'll have to tell Uncle Jerry. He gets a kick out of proving people wrong. He's not shy about working out in public—rest areas or places like this. If there's room, he exercises."

"I didn't expect him to be…a marine."

"If I'd told you that about him, would that have made a difference?" she whispered, pulling one of the last packages of powdered doughnuts off the shelf.

The conversation seemed almost normal—or as normal as his life got. Bree was excited to see her uncle, but Jake had a creepy feeling tying his guts in knots. A feeling like he was being watched. It was bad enough that he wanted to put his back against a wall and come out fighting.

He'd dealt with the strain of going against orders—sort of. Going against his principles by breaking the law was worse with his conscience. But if he'd followed his instincts those last four months in the marines, he might have… He couldn't play the "what if" game any more than Bree should. He'd given her the same advice that he lived by. That's how you got through the beginning days and the only way it got easier as time dragged on.

"Jerry just wants to help," she said in a low voice.

If she spoke much lower, he'd have to bend to her height to hear. The truck stop was crowded with people and chaotic noise. The café was packed with stranded motorists camping in every available corner. No one was leaving. The same was true for the store. The shelves were being depleted of food since the highway had been closed for going on eight hours.

It was worse than an airport with stranded travelers.

"We stick with the plan. If we're stuck here while the road's closed, he's right, we should get some rest. He'll keep watch so we can."

"He could come with us and leave the phone with one of his friends."

"Do you trust them like you do your uncle? We stick

with the plan and take control of the situation by getting your family to safety. Then we go to the police. That's the deal. We can't fight an unknown enemy. Agreed?"

She abruptly nodded and picked up some oversize gloves. "You're one proud marine, Jake Craig. Too proud, if you ask me."

The feeling of being watched intensified. He kept his head down looking at a portable heater for a car, pretending to read the details but looking around him at all the possibilities. He'd have no problem recognizing the kid who'd shot him.

There were a lot of people around, but most were staying put, not wandering the aisles. Not many—if any—had arrived after them, either. Maybe the fear of being caught off guard again was just making him paranoid. There was a strong possibility that Larry and the kid hadn't made it as far north as he and Bree. He needed to make her understand that it wasn't his pride unwilling to accept help.

He tapped her shoulder and she raised her purple eyes to his. Her skin was clear with a spattering of freckles across a straight nose. He wanted to stroke the bruise he'd heard Larry give her before pure rage that anyone had flawed her skin rushed through his veins. He had to cap it and let the anger go.

"If I were you, I'd probably be listening to my uncle, too. You've known him longer. But you have to trust that I know what I'm doing." And won't make any more mistakes like the previous day. "What we're doing isn't for public knowledge. I'm willing to break the law to help get your family to safety, but if we accept help from your uncle, then he could go to jail. I don't think you want that."

"It's nice to see a familiar face, that's all."

"I know how you feel." But he was looking for a young, chunky face that could barely shave. Sifting through all the noise for a rough voice he'd heard only once on the phone. And hoping that the GPS phone would ring so he could get Bree away from all these witnesses and just kiss her senseless.

He had to be as tired as Jerry had proved with that punch to think about kissing her in the middle of all this chaos.

"Do you? How?"

"Hmm?" He shook his head. He'd forgotten what she was asking. The man two aisles over turned his face to avoid eye contact or so he couldn't get a look. Time to go. "Let's pay for this stuff."

"What's wrong?"

His arm was around her shoulders and he got a good grip on her before she could react. He didn't resist sliding a finger over her bruised cheek. Then he tilted her chin toward him to keep her from searching the room, leaning close to her ear as he whispered, "I think the guy in the black coat and stocking cap a couple of rows behind me has been shadowing us around the store. We're paying for our snacks and walking outside. Can you do that without being weird?"

"Sure."

"Good. 'Cause I don't want him to have any idea about what hits him when he rounds the far corner."

"He's coming over here," she said, her lips inches from his.

If they hadn't been in the middle of a hundred people, stuck in the middle of a blizzard whiteout with two murderous bastards on their heels…well, he might have kissed her then and there.

"Pardon me?"

Jake spun around, keeping Bree behind him. The guy

was young all right, but his face was drawn and more slender than the man who'd shot him.

"What?" Jake snapped. His adrenaline was on overdrive along with every sensual cell in his body that he knew about and some that he didn't. The guy's face looked embarrassed. "Sorry, you caught me off guard."

"I'm the one who's sorry, man. I guess I've hit up everybody else in this place, but I'm trying to hitch a ride west when the storm breaks."

"Can't help you there." Bree tugged on Jake's sleeve and he dug some bills out of his pocket. "This might help."

"I don't want no charity, man."

"Someone gave me a break once. Pass it on when the time's right."

He smiled, took the money, said thanks and left. Jake barely heard him. The GPS phone was vibrating.

"THIS IS CRAIG."

Bree listened to the one-sided conversation, glad Jake didn't lose his cool telling Larry the murderer they were staying in Wichita Falls. The conversation only had two or three sentences. Jake kept her against his back while, she guessed, he kept an eye out for a man on a cell phone. That's what she would have been looking for if she could see over the rows of items for sale.

"Come on, let's get out of here," he said, guiding her elbow to the counter.

They zipped their jackets while the cashier totaled their doughnuts, milk and gum. Her heart was just beating normally again when they pushed their way through the door. Each step was a struggle. Not only did they have to walk through the snowdrifts, but each time one foot was off the ground, the wind gusted to blow her to one side.

They got to the rig and her uncle took the dogs to the

truck so he could keep watch. He had everything ready for them to rest in the sleeper section.

"I have had serious bed envy over the past couple of months. And let me tell you, none of them looked as good as that thin mattress and old, thick comforter." She pulled her jacket off, then her shoes, and had every intention of stripping the uncomfortable wet jeans off, too.

Warmth was definitely more important than modesty.

"Bed envy?" Jake asked from the driver's seat, where he was peeling his hat and gloves off.

"I've been sleeping in a different bed every four or five days for several months."

"Or not sleeping in one at all when you sat at the diner. I get it."

"I wanted to crawl into yours so badly last night." Too late she realized what she'd implied. "Not that I meant while you were in bed, 'cause you weren't while we were there. Dallas was and that's why I was even looking."

"I understand, Bree." He smiled and rubbed his jaw, then used his nails to scratch near his sideburn. "Think Dallas will be okay with Jerry? She seemed to like Charlie good enough."

Short, manly nails rubbing across manly beard stubble on a manly, square jawline.... Her insides turned to mush. He stopped and looked at her as if she might just be crazy. "I'm sorry. What? I must be really tired."

"We both are. Is that door locked?" He was taking his time getting his boots unlaced and off his feet.

She was ready to shimmy out of her jeans and put her head on a pillow. Once her eyes were closed she wouldn't put her foot in her mouth so easily. At least she hoped not to step all over her words.

Jake leaned back against the window and closed his eyes. Now was her chance. She quickly unzipped and scooted and pulled, peeling each leg out of the denim. Now she wouldn't get the bed soaking wet. She rotated to get between the cab seats and took a quick glance toward the driver's seat.

Hot brown eyes burned her skin as he looked her over from her hip to her ankle and back again. "That probably wasn't a great idea."

"Nope." Jake's Adam's apple visibly moved.

Why she was paralyzed she didn't know. He took another long, smoldering stare, not bothering to hide it. How was it possible for brown eyes to look so hot? Or for her skin, so cold a few moments before, to feel on fire when he hadn't touched her at all?

"Night." His voice was low and hoarse. And, more than anything else, sexy.

"Good night, Jake."

She moved her left foot toward the bed and a single finger circled her right hip bone, stopping both her movement and her heart. The same nail she'd envied moments before skimmed the length of her leg like a butterfly. So soft she wondered if she was imagining it.

Her heart jump-started again, pounding, questioning what should come next or if *anything* would come next. Her mind told her to wrap herself tight in those covers and forget he was in the sleeper cab. But her body had reacted to him from the first moment she'd seen him twenty-four hours earlier.

It was too soon. Then why was his finger still taunting her skin? Was he asking permission? Wondering what she'd do?

She wanted the answer to that question, too. Unable to move forward, unable to tell him to stop. She barely knew him. But she'd lived more in one day at his side than she had in the past two years alone.

She captured his hand closing in on her hip again. He didn't pull away. She didn't push him away. She closed her eyes, breathing deeply and letting the warmth of his palm soak into her skin again.

Then she laced her fingers through his, not letting go as she lay between the covers and tugged him into the sleeper with her.

Chapter Eighteen

"I don't think this is what your uncle had in mind when he told us to get some rest." He smiled at her, staying on his knees, giving her time to reconsider.

Their first kiss at his apartment didn't encourage her to reconsider. She wanted to take advantage of the storm and their break in this madness.

"Shh. Don't talk. Don't think."

Exhausted from listening to her head and pushing her heart aside, she slid her fingertip across his lips until the fire returned to his eyes. She dragged her nails down his sweater and warmed her hands against his tight undershirt against his abs.

He crossed his arms and a moment later the soft wool was tossed to the front seat. "There's not much room back here."

"I think we'll fit."

Her hands tugged a moment at the white cotton, but he delayed her, reaching to the small of his back. He unhooked his gun holster and laid it to the side of the pillow. Shifting, he straddled her legs, removed his shirt, belt and moved to his jeans.

"Wait." She took his hands away from the zipper. "There's something I've been dying to do."

Back in his apartment, he'd casually walked around

shirtless. This moment wasn't her first glimpse of his muscles and tight abs or the first time she'd longed to get his hot skin next to hers. But it was her first contact and she planned on enjoying it. She wasn't disappointed. His heat shot through her palms as she slowly caressed each curve and hard contour.

Jake could have melted those snowdrifts if he'd just taken his shirt off. The burning under her hands intensified with each pass across his chest. There wasn't an ounce of soft on him.

It would have been easy to let her eyes close and just feel. Let his hands have their way and start the intimate exploring. But watching *his* eyes close and hearing *his* sharp hiss between *his* clenched teeth as she ran her fingers along the top of his jeans…it made the anticipation of his exploration even more intense.

She was glad the diesel engine had the entire truck humming as much as her body. The small vibration hid the quiver shooting through her. She didn't want Jake to feel guilty or question this moment later—today, tomorrow or days from now. He wasn't taking advantage of her emotions or their fatigue. Whatever happened later between them happened. She had no illusions.

But she also knew the risks of not loving when you could. What if she went to jail and never had the opportunity to love again? What if something went wrong with the rescue and she wasn't around at all?

Making love was her question to ask. Her choice to make. Jake had already given his consent. She unzipped his fly, feeling his power as she peeled the jeans down to his knees. She saw him stretched to capacity and they hadn't truly touched yet. He leaned forward, his arms to either side of her, demonstrating the control he had by kicking out of one pants leg and then the other. He didn't touch her. She longed to arch her back or wrap her arms around his neck, pulling him to her breasts.

After the jeans joined the other clothing in the front seat, Jake pushed back to his previous straddle. His last article of clothing did little to hide his desire. The jolt of longing kicking its way through her insides was driving her crazy. The man who had saved her more than once today, leaned to one side, tugging slowly at the comforter she'd been hiding under.

It was still her choice to move forward or pull the covers back to her chin. She allowed them to glide past her hips. He used the back of his finger, dragging it along the bottom of her T-shirt, then along her ribs and the curve of her breast. She thought she'd died right then and there, but he drew more circles on the inside of her arm, across her belly, along her neck—everywhere except where she wanted him the most.

"Your turn to lose the shirt," that deep voice said, thick with lust. "Need help?"

Was it just lust?

No.

Jake Craig could have seduced her in the shower, could have coaxed her to his comfortable bed. Instead, he'd fought icy roads and high winds to get her closer to rescuing her family. Even now, he skimmed the outside of her shirt, raising the edge, skittering across her skin to make her ache with need.

This humble marine turned detective had given up so much to help her. He'd pushed forward through a blizzard. He might have threatened her with jail, but he'd sent a detailed shopping list with her sizes for new clothes. And every step of the way, he'd listened to her opinion and thoughts.

There was a strong possibility she was falling for this guy and they had kissed once.

Remedying their lack of kissing should be easy. She put her hands on his shoulders and brought his hard body down to hers. But Jake had his own idea and slid one hand under her waist, arching her back to expose her neck.

A sigh escaped her when their hips finally connected. It wasn't enough. The weight of him felt protective and she wanted more. Her fingers seized his flexing biceps, wanting to push them aside and have him crash onto her.

He teased her flesh by tipping her head back and caressing her jawline with his lips. He got closer, his kisses hotter, but when she turned her lips toward him, he'd dart to the flesh on the inside of her arm. He continued his playful toying down her neck and across the tops of her breasts.

How long did he think she could take this exquisite abuse?

"Ready to lose this shirt yet?" he asked.

Her shirt came off with the barest break in his torturous touching. He was building a bonfire and she was the wood. Each stroke added another bit of fuel just waiting for a spark. His hands skimmed over her nipples, almost ignoring them, making them ache for a wild grasp right until the palm of his hand scorched her belly.

And then…the shyest of touches on the outside of her panties. Her heart pounded at just the thought. If his hands weren't skimming, touching or cupping, his lips were. She didn't want to be on the edge of this flame by herself and did a little of her own skimming, but the place Jake was taking her was within her grasp.

"Go on," he whispered into her ear. His lips continued down her jaw and he dipped his head toward her shoulder.

Her hands darted out to bring his face to hers. As her body exploded, his lips enveloped hers. Strong and just right. Everything about it was as perfect as she'd known it would be.

If the two of them had been smoldering since their chance encounter at the diner and he'd built her bonfire on top of the embers, then their kiss was the ignition switch.

There was no slow left for either of them. Wild, demanding kisses and strokes that left them with the covers tangled around their ankles. The chill in the air didn't matter. Encased in Jake's heat, Bree could only think of getting closer to his burning skin, becoming a part of him completely and staying there. The more she thought about it, the warmer she became.

He shifted to his side to lean on his elbow. His eyes were dark, and the furrow was back between his eyebrows. He lightly rubbed that serious spot on his forehead.

"You're thinking again."

"I feel like I've been waiting a lifetime to see you naked. You are so damn beautiful, Sabrina Watkins."

"And that makes you worry?"

"It's hard for me to remember we've only known each other twenty-four hours." *And that you should be handed over to authorities.*

"Does that make a difference?" she asked, dragging a finger across his chest. Making him forget even more.

"Maybe it should, but it doesn't." He twirled a strand of her hair around his pinky, leaving it curled as it unwound and dropped next to her tiny ear. He could spend hours taking her body to different sensual levels.

"I know," she whispered before dragging his mouth back to hers. He was ready to kiss more than just her luscious lips.

Before he got crazy with Bree again, he needed the condom from his jeans that he'd picked up inside the truck stop. He'd known—or hoped—this would happen as soon as Jerry suggested grabbing some shut-eye together.

Reluctantly, he backed away from the woman in his arms and dug through his jeans. The snow was still coming down and the wind still moved the truck from side to side. It was the first time he noticed the curtains for the sleeper. He flipped on a small mounted lamp, pulled the curtains and created an intimate cocoon.

The awaiting butterfly still needed to shed one more layer. The frilly black bra hadn't been replaced by something practical from his list. It was hers. The one she'd been wearing since they'd met.

Crazy that it had been one day.

Crazier still was the way he wanted this woman. He wanted her with a fierce hunger and couldn't understand why. He didn't need to understand. She clearly wanted his body, as well.

The back of her hand skimmed across the front of his skivvies when he returned. He pressed toward her fingers, straining to be skin to skin. He used his hand in much the same way and received a sigh and tingle from Bree. Her hands roamed his body and he let his hands roam, too. He lightly traced the lace cups and her pulse leaped in her throat.

Watching her come to life and enjoy his exploring had taken him to a level of sensuality he hadn't experienced before and didn't want to rush. But this was definitely torture.

Time to unsnap the bra and kiss more of Bree's skin. He slid the cups down, releasing the most perfect pair of breasts he'd set eyes on. His mouth followed what his eyes had devoured in a heartbeat. His lips locked on her cool nipple, making it pebble while the other warmed in his hand.

He looped his finger in the material at her hip, a gentle

tug on one side of the thong and—without intending to—the delicate sides snapped. Bree giggled. And his mouth jumped into a smile at the sound.

As bold and comfortable as he became with Bree, she became with him. She matched him touch for touch, stroke for stroke, kiss for kiss. Her body's need was matching his, too. No question about it as she reached for the condom.

Bree surprised him with long, gliding strokes before rolling it on. The tension and heat rose within him and her, if her breath was any indication. She lay back on the mattress, ready, waiting.

No more waiting.

The small space had its advantages. It might not be the sexiest place to make love but he didn't care. He braced himself with one locked arm and slid the other to the small of her back and lifted her, sliding home. Her eyes closed and her mouth opened on a long sigh as she surrounded every inch of him.

Lying next to her, exploring her body…all fine and good. None of that compared to connecting to her. Being complete with her. Rushing to a place that only the two of them could get to together. No, it was more than just *good*.

Why he wanted that connection and with this particular woman—well, he wasn't wondering about it too much. He needed to be closer, dropped to cover her, feel soft skin next to his.

Finishing would be easy, but he'd make sure Bree was satisfied and then satisfied a second time. With slow, even strokes, he loved her. Her hands gripped his shoulders and her body met his, thrust for thrust. The pace picked up, as did their breathing. A moment later her body tightened and she cried out. He caught her hands in his and kept on going.

Inside her was a warm cocoon of its own. She wrapped her legs around him and kept him close. If the wind hadn't hidden the rocking motion of the tractor, then no one would have had any doubts of what was happening inside. The small berth locked the world out, intensifying her softness, her smell, his need. With a few last strokes, they both cried out in fulfillment.

He rolled to his side and caught her to him, barely catching his breath before the scent of his shampoo in her hair made him stiffen again. He wanted more than one morning in her arms. He'd thought he was crazy before. Now there was no doubt.

The magical first moment was over and he waited for reality to burst back on the scene. Waited for Bree to move away. But she didn't.

When her breathing slowed, she faced him, pulled his mouth to hers and he kissed her lips like the first and last time all melted together. She curled her fist against his chest and in two shakes was asleep.

How could he have thought sharing sex would lessen the need for her? Once would never be enough. It wasn't even enough for the moment. There needed to be a *lot* more moments between them. He used the back of a finger to softly caress the darkening cheekbone where she'd been hit by her abductors. He skimmed her breasts and her breathing hitched, wakening her from her light sleep. His hand wandered over her tight belly and then lower.

"We should probably get some shut-eye," she said with an anticipated sigh. "You were…um…pretty tired before the workout."

"Tired before you took your pants off and I saw how little that tiny thong actually covered." He tucked a strand of almost black hair behind her ear and remembered a box of dark hair dye. "I was thinking I should probably know what your real hair color is."

There was one way to satisfy his curiosity and to start another *moment*.

"I've dyed it darker than...oh..."

They could sleep soon, but first, he needed to see for himself.

Chapter Nineteen

Something was different.

Jake woke to darkness and a warm body in his arms. That *was* different. He hadn't had a woman in his bed since before his last tour began. But there was something more.

He was with Bree in the sleeper of Jerry's big rig, behind a heavy curtain. Light snuck through the edges a little brighter than it had when the sun came up.

Storm raging, at different times, they'd pulled most of their clothes back on to be ready to go. He missed the warm smoothness of Bree's skin under his fingers and missed her nails lightly scraping his flesh.

Lying next to her still felt good. She fit. He needed someone who fit. Maybe… The "maybe" dangled in front of him, taunting. Challenging him to jump forward and grab it. Those kind of thoughts were for someone with a future. They wouldn't have one if he didn't clear her name. Even then, the woman in his arms knew nothing of his past. Nothing about the nightmares of war. And he knew nothing about how to tell her.

Now, he needed to concentrate on what had changed.

The diesel still hummed. The noise level from the wind wasn't as loud. He'd swear that the swaying had died down to almost nothing. Both cells vibrated at his head. He'd kept them close in case they rang, but they were both out of his reach unless he moved the sleepyhead off his shoulder. The limited space in the sleeper kept him from claiming Bree's lips first thing like he wanted. He settled for her forehead.

"Bree, time to go." He stretched as best he could and pulled a curtain back to him, filling the small area with bright sunshine.

No snow blowing sideways.

The wind hadn't just slowed down. It had barreled to a racing halt.

"You okay?" Bree asked, pushing up and leaning on her forearm. "Holy smokes, is that the freeway? The storm's over. You're right, it is time to get moving."

Different. He liked different. He patted the bed around his head, searching for the closest phone to answer. She reached over him, her breast flattening against his chest, starting a desire that couldn't be finished…at the moment.

"Here." She handed him his cell. "It's Jerry."

He sat and slammed the phone to his ear, ready to join the game again. "Yeah?"

"Someone's got eyes on your truck." He put it on speaker for Bree to hear as she gathered their shoes in the front seat. "I'm not inside the vehicle. I'm walking the dogs between the third and fourth row of rigs to keep an eye on things. How long do you need?"

"I'll be right out."

"Unwise. They can see my tractor. I don't think they know you're inside. You should keep it that way. Start by getting Sabrina away from the windows."

"Three minutes." Jake disconnected and grabbed Bree under the arms to yank her back to the sleeper—surprised face and all.

She scooted to the opposite side, shoving her feet into

the rubber boots she'd retrieved. "What are you going to do? What happens in three minutes."

"I'm pulling my shoes on and making certain you understand the rules." He pushed his head through the black sweater. He'd be a sitting duck, easily spotted against the snow, but he had nothing else.

"What rules?"

He laced his boots quickly while looking only at Bree. "You aren't going to want to follow my orders, but your uncle and I both need you to stay put. Here. Safe."

"But I can help—"

"I'm better going solo. I'll verify if the men watching the truck are Larry and that young sidekick of his. If they are, I can deal with them. And don't forget, your uncle's out there, too. The last thing we need is to worry about you."

"I've been taking care of myself since this thing all blew up."

"And that's turned out great. You're a distraction if I have to worry about protecting you. Remember, it's you they're after. You're the only person who can give them what they want."

He could tell that his words were getting her peeved. She sat Indian-style with her arms closed around her. An apology was on the tip of his tongue. It was the truth. She was a lovely distraction but a distraction nonetheless. And he couldn't do his job if he was distracted.

"They shot you."

He shifted to her side, pulled the curtain back to the center so no one could see her and kissed her like he'd wanted to when they'd first woken up. He had to rein it in before he had them back under the covers, naked and forgetting about the world.

"Nice jab, but it was just a graze. Won't even leave a

scar as a reminder." He leaned his forehead against hers, tempted to kiss her again, but he needed to get to her uncle.

"Do you have other reminders?"

Several images of early this morning clamored for time in his mind. He didn't think he was likely to forget any part of this weekend adventure and he didn't want to think about the scars he did have from the past eight years. That was a part of him he was determined to forget.

The past was the past. *Former* marine. *Former* life. The scars were there, old wounds that had healed. It was dangerous to go down that path. And dangerous if he kissed her again. What he needed was to get outside and watch the men who thought they were watching him.

"I've got to go. Can you peek through the curtain and take a look at the man leaning on the SUV?" She peeked out as he pulled the laces tight on his second boot. "Recognize him?"

She shook her head. "Jake—"

"I really need that promise, hon." Her purple eyes were going to be his downfall. If one tear fell, he'd…he'd handcuff her to the steering wheel, that's what he'd do. "Promise me."

"I…" The violet orbs darted back and forth between his. "I'll promise you if you promise not to get *grazed* again."

"It seems I've given you a false impression about my capabilities, darlin'. I had a run of bad luck yesterday, but I'm pretty good at what I do."

He withdrew his weapon from its holster and tossed the worn leather in the seat before checking his ammo. Then he bent as low as possible for someone over six feet tall and shifted to the passenger seat to dial her uncle.

"Jerry, got a ninety-second distraction?"

"Oorah." Jerry disconnected.

"What do I do if things don't go like you've planned?" she asked.

"Did I say I have a plan?"

Raised voices from the parking lot. There was his diversion. "Is our Peeping Tom on the corner moving away?"

"Looks like it." She leaned forward and kissed his cheek. "Seriously, Jake. Please be careful."

Somehow that felt as sexy as anything that had happened earlier. Okay, maybe not anything. He slipped out the door and sloshed to level ground where the snow wasn't as deep as the shallow ditch next to the road. There were snowdrifts taller than his head next to buildings.

The whiteout might have ceased, but it would still take hours to get the roads clear of the mess it had left behind. Running through this snow was like running in a thigh-high ocean surf. A terrific workout, but tiring.

What they needed was a chopper. Expensive, but he didn't see any way to lose the men tailing them. Or a way to get to Amarillo fast. They were running out of time to save Bree's family.

If they hadn't already.

There wasn't any real running through the snow, but he moved as quickly as he could, darting behind a post to re-assess his opponent. He should have asked Mac for some winter camouflage so his dark jacket didn't stick out. But the closer he got, the more familiar the man watching his truck became. The same young hitchhiker he'd given a hundred-dollar bill to earlier that morning tried not to be obvious about his actions, but he was definitely watching the truck.

His phone vibrated. Jerry. "You stand out like a tick on a white dog sloshing through that snow. You recognize that fella?"

"He's not one of the men who attacked us at the lake, but he's watching the truck, all right."

"I'll be close."

Jake chased several things from his mind. He liked Bree's uncle Jerry. He also liked Bree—a lot. Maybe too much in such a short period of time. Heck, they already shared a dog. He pushed those thoughts aside and concentrated on his surroundings.

There were more tractors and trailers than he could count. All had their engines running—just like Jerry's. Instead of parking front to back in a straight line, these rigs were side by side. If he could get to higher ground, up top, then he'd be able to see all the movement in both this lot and the truck stop across the street. He pulled himself up between the cab and trailer.

Once he had a good grip, he used his upper body strength. On the roof he dropped to his belly, apparently not the only one with the idea to get a bird's-eye view. A familiar black jacket was perched on the opposite end, five trailers away.

No time to warn Jerry or Bree about his plan—if he could call taking this man down no matter the cost a plan. He pulled his weapon. Once he stood and ran, there wouldn't be anything other than adrenaline pumping through him.

If he could take him alive…great. But that action wasn't high on his priority list. From where the guy was lying, he didn't think Jerry was visible. And where Bree sat on the passenger side of his tractor wasn't.

Surprise was all he had going for him. Jake slid on his belly from the front of the trailer roof to the back, keeping his weapon above the snow and ice. His hands were frozen, but he couldn't pull the trigger wearing gloves. He blew on his right fingers, rubbing and warming before he stood.

The man still hadn't seen or heard him. He could thank the diesel engines for drowning out most of the noise. A couple of quick inhales and he took off, thankful he wore the military boots that kept him from sliding around as he pushed from one trailer to the next. He jumped the first three-foot space between trailers easily enough, the second wasn't so tough. But after Jake landed the third, the man rolled to his back at the sound.

One more to go.

Shots. He heard the ping of metal midair between four and five. He landed and dropped flat. More shots, but this guy wasn't a good aim. Must be the kid who grazed him at the lake.

"Give it up, kid. Didn't you learn that you can't hit the broadside of a marine?"

The kid scrambled to his knees, scared. He wasn't wearing the ski mask. Sure enough it was Larry's sidekick with the unshaven double chin. Jake jumped to his feet and leaped to the silver roof before another shot came a little too close.

The length of a trailer and a three-foot opening was all that stood between him and taking this wannabe murderer to the police. Right after he supplied Jake with any information he might have about where the Watkins family was being held.

"Come on, kid. You know you aren't getting away from me. Everything badass that you've heard about marines… imagine that and add a little more…then you'll get me." It was the part of him he wanted to bury and never resurrect, but the kid didn't know that.

The kid's gun hand shook and it wasn't from the cold. "Y-y-you c-can't do n-n-nothin' to me. Y-y-you're a c-cop," he stuttered.

Jake wanted to feel sorry for him. But he didn't. This

kid had joined forces with a murderer and abducted Bree. He still hadn't gotten the full story about what they'd done to her. Neither of the creeps deserved mercy from him.

Think calm. Try not to kill him.

"You shoot me, kid, you're a cop killer. You know what they do to cop killers?" He watched the kid's face go paler. "That's right, it's the death penalty."

"They ain't ever gonna c-c-catch us."

Jake shook his head and purposefully smiled. "Look around you, kid. No one's going *anywhere* soon. How are you going to get away?"

Jake walked slowly to the edge of the trailer, faking the confidence he lacked. He hadn't caught a good look at the type of weapon the kid was using or had any idea how much ammo he carried. They were squared up with about ten feet separating them, three of which had a thirteen-foot drop to the ground.

The kid wasn't moving anything except his eyes. He seemed nervous but frozen in place as much as the ground.

You want this guy alive, a voice nagged at him.

He wants you dead, another shouted.

Taking him into custody wouldn't be easy. Jake wanted him alone. Wanted to give the kid a dose of his own medicine. The trailer shifted just as he was about to make a move. An extra thump or rocking motion shot up his back about the time the kid's mouth slightly rose at the corner in a smirk.

The kid raised his weapon. Confident.

Fire.

"Behind you, Craig!" Jerry yelled from somewhere on the ground.

Larry. The kid's partner stood at the back of the silver trailer. Gun in hand. Aimed at Jake's chest.

Chapter Twenty

Fire.

Jake's weapon didn't waver. He didn't need to cover both men. Larry was the threat.

"Take care of the dog walker before someone else comes around," Larry commanded.

Jerry disappeared around the back ends of the trucks. He hoped one of his "partners" would think now was a good time to call the cops. Naw, Bree wouldn't, but Jerry might. They could keep Bree hidden and out of the police questioning.

"Big, tough m-marine fell for...for the stuttering routine." The kid swallowed hard, his Adam's apple bobbing in his thick neck.

Clearly accepting the orders, the kid dropped clumsily off the orange rooftop and out of sight.

"We got a problem, man," Larry said. "All we need's the girl and the money."

You need this guy alive. Jake knew why he stood there listening to a criminal, but what was Larry's reason to talk it up with a cop? What did they hope to gain?

"So maybe you should shoot that gun in your hand instead of treating it like a toy. Or I could shoot you and resolve both our problems."

Larry shrugged, trying to look tough by smiling, like

every stereotypical bad guy Jake had seen in the movies and rarely encountered on the streets.

Jake wanted to punch the smile right off his face, leaving a mark a hell of a lot worse than the one on Bree's cheek. He'd settle for dislocating the man's jaw. Then he'd dare *Larry* to try to look like…whatever.

"You think you're smart? Thing is, ya shoot me and you know you'll never get her family back. No chance my brother will let 'em go unless you do what I say."

"Yeah, I know. It's the one reason you aren't dead already. So your point, Larry?" It was tempting to pull the trigger and end the smug arrogance of a confessed murderer, but the cop in him was stronger than the shoot-first-and-ask-questions-later. *Alive. You need this guy alive.* He'd keep the man alive and lock him away in jail.

"The point is," Larry said, "I have what you want and you won't shoot me. So drop it."

Barking. A familiar howl. Dallas and Charlie.

"Get 'em off me. Stop." That had to be the kid. "I'll kill her, old man. I'll kill her."

Larry's eyes darted toward the sound of the scuffle. Jake stared at the gun barrel as it drooped. Slightly, but that was enough. Jake squeezed the trigger microseconds before Larry. No longer aiming at a stationary target, Larry missed, then dropped flat to the top of the icy silver trailer, dodging Jake's shot.

Jake jumped to the orange trailer, dug his toes into the ice, keeping his footing on the roof. *Alive. You need this guy alive.* If he hadn't been repeating the line, he would have emptied his clip. But he didn't fire. To his right he caught a glimpse of someone with long, dark hair rolling in the snow, fighting with a man in a black jacket. Just a glimpse as he refocused on Larry, to his left, who was getting to his knees and standing.

Jake raised his arms and leaped across the trailers, smashing Larry to his back and sending both weapons flying. The crash thrust them skidding across the trailer. Jake latched on to his opponent's jacket. He dug his steel-toed boots into the icy silver roof to slow their slide. His feet caught on a roof reinforcement, stopping them from plunging over the side.

Larry threw his arm across Jake's windpipe, pushing, acting unconcerned that they both might teeter over the trailer's edge. Hitting the ground headfirst—snow or no snow—could be deadly.

"What now, cop?" he said, clenching his jaw and shoving harder.

Another impasse. They'd have to roll to their sides and let go of each other in order to get to their feet. How could he take this maniac alive?

The double-chinned kid backed around the corner of the semi, shoving Bree. Her arm was twisted behind her back with his gun pointed straight at her temple.

Jerry was nowhere in sight.

"Let him go or I'll kill her!" the kid shouted. "But don't drop him. I mean—" Bree stumbled into a snowdrift and the kid began kicking, connecting with her side. She curled into a ball, protecting herself. "I won't stop till you let him go."

"Don't kick her to death. He gets it," Larry said. His face was too close not to miss the "I win" glare in his eyes. "We need her."

The arm crushing Jake's larynx cautiously lifted. Jake rolled and pulled himself back until both of them could grab the side of the truck and catch their balance. They moved apart, rolling in opposite directions and scrambling to their feet. The instant he stood, he saw the challenge in Larry's eyes. His opponent already had a switchblade palmed.

Jake wasn't worried about the aggression. He was through treating these men like they were worth any kindness. Every strike he inflicted wouldn't begin to pay back for what Bree had endured.

Larry thumbed the lever and the blade popped into place. He lunged.

One defensive move at a time, Jake's years of military training took over. Once let loose, there was no stopping the return of the machine he'd never wanted to evoke into action again.

Chapter Twenty-One

Bree's side was on fire from the kicks to her ribs. She haltingly unzipped her jacket without anyone noticing and withdrew one of the guns she'd taken from Jake's black bag. She couldn't see either man on top of the trailer, but she could see her uncle's signal telling her it was time. Hopefully, Jake would benefit from the distraction and be able to save himself. And her. She uncurled and rolled under the edge of the trailer. As soon as the bastard who'd just kicked her leaned down to grab her, she stuck her gun in his face.

"Drop your gun." She spoke softly so only the kid—as Jake had called him—could hear.

When he did, she moved until she could pick it up, then shoved the gun into her pocket. Her uncle came from behind her with packing tape he'd retrieved out of his bottomless pit of road supplies. But her uncle didn't move fast enough. The kid started running, yelling and flailing his arms.

"Larry! Larry! Larry!"

"I'll get him." Jerry came out of hiding. "Find those guns. The cops will be here any minute." He ran through the snow, gaining on the kid.

Bending to look for those guns, the pain in her ribs shot through her like an ice pick. She'd almost felt sorry for the kid, but not so much while she clenched her jaw and got control of her breathing back. Finding those guns was easier said than done. "I don't think anyone's going to find them until this snow melts," she mumbled.

The trailer rocked at her back. Jake fought with Larry again, just as her uncle had predicted. She backed up in the knee-deep snow until she could see the men on the rooftop. A crowd had gathered outside the store across the street and were headed this way.

"Jake! I can hear the police." The siren wailed in the distance. She couldn't be delayed trying to convince them her family was in trouble. They had to get out of there. She looked up in time to see Jake's boot catch Larry in the chest, rocketing him over the back of the trailer toward her.

He landed on his back at a weird angle. They needed him for answers.

"Bree, stop!"

She was already at Larry's side to see if he was dead. His eyes popped open, his hand latched to her arm and toppled her to his chest. Before she blinked there was a knife, nicking her throat.

"No playing this time, princ—"

A loud gunshot stopped Larry's words and knife. Jake tugged on her to get her going. He'd jumped down so fast she hadn't seen him. His mouth moved, but she couldn't understand him through the fog. Larry's eyes were open, a bullet wound to his chest.

"I'm going to be sick."

"Do it over here." Jake pushed her behind him into a snowdrift. "As soon as the crowd gets brave enough, they're going to investigate that last shot. Where's Jerry?"

As much as her stomach objected to the picture fresh in her mind, she didn't lose her cookies. "After the kid, who was running toward the freeway."

She took a step to pass Jake and was enveloped in his arms instead. His gentle touch to her neck was a sharp contrast to the man she'd seen fighting on that trailer. The same man who had shot Larry dead to save her. He tilted her chin, using the pad of his thumb to create those soothing circles.

"Are you okay?" He tilted her head farther. The wet drops of blood where the knife had broken the skin were whisked away.

"I'm fine."

"If we weren't in a hurry..."

"But we are. Where's my uncle and that other murderer?" Bree couldn't think of him as a young man who'd fallen under the wrong guidance. That was for a jury to decide. Right now, she needed to help her family and he was the key. Their only clue.

They took off. Jake had her elbow securely in his strong hand. She wanted to remember his hands from early this morning—gentle, loving. The firm grip was comforting, but it had also pulled the trigger pushing them farther from getting the money to Griffin.

They skirted the oncoming crowd. The police cars made it to the truck stop. She ran, barely keeping up with Jake as he searched for her uncle. Then they both saw the hitchhiker trying to get their attention.

"He's going to kill him. They're behind the trash." His hands were full trying to contain both dogs.

"Stay here," Jake instructed, looking at them both.

"This is my fight," she said to his back, following.

Her uncle was pinned on the ground. The kid hit his arm with a pipe. As he raised it again, Jake grabbed it, hurling the pipe into the bags of excess trash spilling from the receptacles.

The younger man turned his anger on Jake. "I'm not

going back! They promised." He pommeled Jake, who kept retreating, leading him farther away from Jerry.

With the hitchhiker on her heels, she ran to Jerry. "Are you all right?"

She helped him sit and listened not to his explanation but for sounds of another fight.

"I think my arm's busted." He cradled his left wrist in his thick hand. "The boy caught me by surprise. I turned right into that pipe and went down like a sinker on a fishing pole."

"Can you stay with him?" she asked the man holding their dogs. She and her uncle had "hired" him to dog sit with the promise of a ride to California when they'd concocted their plan to keep Jake from being shot.

"Take one of these things, will ya?"

Dallas squirmed out of his arms and into hers, licking her hands, glad to see her. She set her on the ground and put her leash back in the young man's hand.

"I love you, Uncle Jerry." She rose, ran in the direction Jake had led the fight and listened for sounds. When she didn't hear any, she backed up to the corner of a small building and waited.

She should have stayed with her uncle. Things had moved so fast. Her first thought had been to help Jake. How in the world could she do that? Screaming for help was the last thing she could do. The police were in the parking lot. People in the crowd had to have seen them running from Larry's body.

Her stomach lurched at the image of the bullet hole and blood on the snow.

"Where's the money?"

At first she thought the person was asking her. Then she realized the kid Jake chased was around the corner of the building.

"Man, I told you. She said Amarillo. That's all I know," Jake lied.

He knew the money was in his bag of black op equipment. If she could get the gun she had into Jake's hands, then he could capture the kid. She pulled the gun from her pocket and knelt on the ground.

"I don't know what to do. Where's Larry?"

"Want me to take you to him, man? I can do that."

She looked around the corner, straight into Jake's jeans. She could almost tug on his hand and place the gun in his fingers. He took a step forward, his hand out of her reach.

She stood, leaning against the stucco building, holding the gun in both hands just like she'd been taught. But she'd also been taught not to point a loaded weapon at a person. Life or death made it different. She'd get the kid to drop the knife, Jake would be safe and they'd find out about her family.

"Hold it," she said, barreling around the corner, gun aimed at both men.

"Ahhh!" the kid screamed, knife raised, lunging for Jake.

"Stay back, Sabrina!"

Jake's defensive moves were textbook perfect. He countered the downward thrust of the knife with a sweeping block of his forearm. He caught the kid's wrist in his hand and shook. Pinned in the snowdrift, their legs barely moved as Jake released the kid's opposite shoulder to grab the arm with the knife.

The kid pressed forward, wild-eyed and hysterical. He yanked his arm free from Jake's grasp, violently shoving and wildly wielding the knife from side to side. "I'll kill her. I'll kill her."

Jake growled and blocked the descent of the blade. Bree realized she still aimed the gun at them both. She shoved it back in her pocket, knowing she wouldn't shoot. They couldn't risk killing their only lead to her family.

Each assault from the younger man was countered by the more experienced ex-marine. The kid's wielding of the knife became more frantic and chaotic as he tried to get past Jake.

Their attacker kept crying out, "I have to kill her. I have to kill her." His words hypnotized Bree at the building corner. She was unable to move or cry out or help. Her uncle came around the corner and darted forward without hesitation, broken wrist and all.

There was a final sweep of Jake's arm, the knife disappeared, a scream and then the kid threw back his head and collapsed in the snow. While Jake and Jerry looked at his wound, trying to stanch the blood, she ran over and took the young man's face in her hands. His eyes focused far from her. She shook his coat collar to get his attention, losing whatever bit of decency she had left.

"Who are you working for? Where's my family? Tell me!" Her uncle could have died. What if Jake had died for her?

"You won't get—" He coughed. A bead of dark red blood dropped from his nose. "They promi…"

She stumbled back into Jake's stable body.

Her uncle checked for a pulse and confirmed what was evident from the glazed, open eyes.

"They're…dead. Both dead?" She started breathing and talking fast, unable to block all the unanswered questions filling her head.

"It'll be okay," Jake said, from just above her ear, leading her back toward the truck.

"Can't you see he's dead? Did he say where my family is being held? Who he works for? Why did you kill him? You killed them both. It's all your fault."

"*My* fault?" Jake answered, leaning on the truck, breathing a little hard. "Damn, why didn't I stop to interrogate him? Oh, yeah, he was beating your uncle with a steel pipe. Then he was determined to kill you and me with a knife. I saved your uncle. And I saved you. Totally unnecessary if you'd stayed in the truck."

She knew she was wrong and still the fear bubbled to the surface in the form of spiteful words. "What about my mother, father and sister? What if these two have to report to Griffin? And when they don't? What happens when Griffin knows his men are dead. It'll be all over the news before we can possibly get near Amarillo."

"Try to calm down, Bree. You're in shock." Jake pulled her face to his shoulder, muffling the sounds of her sobs. "We'll find a way. Don't give up. Right now we've got to get out of here."

"Give her the black dog," Jerry told the hitchhiker. "Bree, you and Jake need to get out of here before the police head this way."

"Are we getting out of here, too?" the hitchhiker asked, setting the dogs in the snow.

"All in due time," her uncle answered.

"Dallas should stay with you," Jake told him.

She shook her head. "She's *my* dog. You can't give her to anyone."

Burying her face in the dog's cold fur, she had little faith they'd succeed and paid no attention as she was pushed into the truck. The engine started, Jake barreled through the snow away from the crowds, two dead bodies and the police stuck trying to determine what had happened.

"I don't know how my uncle thinks he's going to talk his way out of jail."

"If you'd stayed in the truck—"

"You'd be dead," she answered quickly.

"Dammit, Bree. You broke your promise to stay in the truck. Don't blame me for having to clean up the mess."

"You really expected me to just sit there and not fight for myself?"

"Yes."

"Then I'm not sure why you're even trying to get away or continue to help me. It's hopeless."

"We aren't beaten yet, Bree. I've seen hopeless, and this isn't one of those scenarios."

She tucked Dallas into the dog bed in the backseat. She couldn't look at Jake, no matter how encouraging he was attempting to be, so she dropped her face into her hands. Yes, he saved her life with his accurate shot, but at what price? "They're dead, aren't they? My family. All of my family's gone and it's my fault."

"Never think that. Griffin knows he needs them alive to get the money back."

"It's a long way to Amarillo. We can't just snap our heels together and get there in an instant. And then we have to find them. And rescue them. Driving, it's three and a half hours on a good day. Just admit that it's impossible to save them."

"I promise you, sweetheart, we're getting to your family before anything happens. It's only two hours by chopper. They won't be expecting us. We'll have leverage and surprise on our side."

A hint of the look she'd seen while he'd fought crowded the features she adored and had kissed so hungrily less than an hour ago. She couldn't possibly be attracted to the fighter he'd unleashed on those two men, but she needed those killer instincts to win this battle.

"Just tell me what to do."

Was there a fighter left in her? She'd been running so long, afraid of failing, afraid of no one believing in her.

Had the past years of building her business against the advice of her friends and family meant nothing? Could she remember what it was like to fight for what she wanted?

Chapter Twenty-Two

Sometime during one of his encounters today, Jake's side had been sliced by a knife. Not a bad wound, but enough blood to show through his sweater. Bree had accused him of keeping the cut a secret, but he honestly didn't remember it happening.

No helicopters had been available and it had taken a lot longer for a charter pilot to get there than he'd hoped. He'd been anticipating the police finding them before they could get the runway cleared and their plane in the air. Five thousand dollars later, they still had a good hour before reaching Amarillo.

All he wanted to do was nap. His sore jaw reminded him he needed to be alert and at his best. But the look in Bree's eyes wasn't restful. His clean T-shirt was off, his side had been washed and he waited while she searched through the pilot's first-aid kit for antiseptic.

The atmosphere inside the cabin was still freezing. Bree had stopped talking, using gestures instead of words. At least with him. He didn't like it, wanting to wrap his arms around her and haul her to his lap. He wanted to forget the faces, his actions. Wanted her to believe everything he did was to keep her safe.

"Finding this plane is better than a noisy helicopter." He

settled for random conversation instead. "Easier to stretch my legs."

He extended his long limbs into the aisle as Bree rested between their seats on one knee, cleaning his wound. The plane pitched in the air and she wobbled. When he reached out to steady her, she jerked away.

"I don't feel right using any of that money for this plane."

"We didn't have much of a choice. It was the only charter available and Ernie wanted three thousand cash up front before he'd fly." Her delicate fingers were warm and soothing against his skin. Her gentle touch was worth the alcohol sting on the laceration.

She balanced in the aisle and worked in her seat as the plane sped forward. A picture of her bare thigh and the thong he'd torn came to him. He'd love to get his hands on that black lace bra again.

"I think you need stitches." She had the gauze and tape in hand and ready to go when the plane dipped quickly and she lost her balance heading nose first to the floor.

Jake steadied her around her ribs, forgetting that she'd been kicked by the kid. Their pilot recovered with a few curses and a message of "Sorry, folks." Bree twisted from his grasp.

"Are you in a lot of pain?" he asked. He didn't think it was just her injury keeping his hands off her. He'd seen that disgusted look before.

"Only when I lean hard on something."

"Or if someone grabs you." He looked at his injury. "I'll be fine with no stitches. Tear some of that tape into half-inch strips."

She began and he gritted his teeth before pulling his wound closed tight. "If you...um...put the tape on and...

yeah, draw it together. Just like that. Now the gauze. Great. See, no stitches needed."

"You still need a doctor."

"I'm all caught up on my shots." It wasn't his imagination—she got away from him as fast as possible. "I've had many a scratch taped like this. No trips to Emergency for me when I was growing up."

"You can't be serious." She sat and pulled Dallas onto her lap. "Why would your parents do that?"

"My grandmother, actually. She took care of me summers. Stitches were equivalent to being stuck in the house. So she'd tape me back together, I'd go play outside and she had peace."

"My grandmother's the reason I started my business. I'd walk her dog and bathe it. My uncle moved back after his discharge and her dogs did wonders for him. Charlie was amazing helping him work through his PTSD. When I got older, I house-sat. My granny connected me to friends in Amarillo for summers. Seemed natural to expand my business instead of attending college or working in a coffee shop."

He caught a silent tear on her cheekbone. He could see the withdrawal in her violet eyes as she pulled back from his touch. "Look, I'm sort of getting the impression you'd rather I keep my hands to myself. I thought we were past that but—"

"We moved past it way too fast. No offense, Jake, but I don't know you at all. So maybe we should back up a little."

"You want to pretend this morning didn't happen?"

"I wish I could pretend none of it happened."

"None of it?"

"Why would I want to remember those two men being killed?"

Or him killing them. "I get it."

"I know you did what you thought was best."

He needed out of here and he didn't see a parachute handy, so he was stuck a foot away from the first person he'd let close since returning from overseas. He'd let a dang puppy break through his defenses and she'd tugged her owner right along with her.

The plane dipped and Bree almost lost the pup out of her hands. "Whoa there, girl."

Dallas squirmed and jumped to his lap, barking a couple of times and ending on a short howl. She climbed Jake's chest and started licking his chin. "That dog going to jump around the whole way?" Ernie asked.

"I should have left her with my uncle. I wasn't thinking straight."

He knew exactly why she'd brought the pup. Comfort. "It's okay. Maybe we can pay Ernie to dog sit."

"Or find another hitchhiker. That was so bizarre. Jerry asked what he was watching, gave him the once-over and then said, 'Boy, I'll give you a ride clear to California if you just hold these dogs for me.'"

"You left your uncle's truck. Before I was almost shot. Why? You promised you wouldn't. I knew I should've used the handcuffs to keep you there."

"I really couldn't sit there letting you fight for me and take all the risks. Besides, I wanted to help you keep your promise that you wouldn't get grazed." She drew a line through his hair above his ear, mirroring the bullet burn from the day before.

He jerked his head away from the pleasant stroke. "No touching works both ways."

Her face changed from relaxed to what-am-I-doing in a heartbeat. "The chubby…guy was following my uncle. I thought he was in trouble. I couldn't stay safe while you were both fighting."

"That's exactly what you should have done."

"Our impromptu plan got you safely off the trailer roof," she defended.

Did your plan include shooting Larry? Even unspoken, the question hung between them. Her eyes darted worriedly back and forth. She knew what he'd almost asked. She bit her lip and drew in a long sigh. She also knew his answer. If she hadn't been in danger, he wouldn't have shot him.

Whatever had taken place in their dark corner of the whiteout this morning had vanished. Just like his ex-wife had needed him for her own purposes, Sabrina Watkins did, too. His place was either as a long-distance husband or the hired help.

He wasn't looking for a permanent relationship. Hell, he wasn't looking for *any* relationship. So what was the big deal about losing this one before it had really begun. *You've only known her for two days.*

"I can hold Dallas while you rest."

He stroked the pup's soft fur and rubbed her tummy when she stretched her paws into the air. "She's fine where she is. You've already discovered I don't share well. Now it's the pup's turn to learn who's boss."

He closed his eyes and was met with another death stare chiseled into his memory. He'd seen too many deaths to count. But he knew. He'd always know the number of people who had lost their lives on his watch. Larry and the kid may have been murderers and trying to kill them, but Jake hated having their deaths on his conscience.

You killed them both. It's all your fault.

He jerked awake, unable to get her words out of his head. He and Jerry had tried to help the kid after he'd deflected the knife into his abdomen, but nothing could be done. He'd washed and washed again before they'd gone wheels up. He would never get all the blood off.

His hands were clean, only figuratively stained. Bree knew it and should keep her distance. She rested her head against the window. He missed her head on his shoulder.

"I should have sent you to jail. You would've been safer."

She rotated to face him within the confines of her seat belt. The plane still pitched in the wind. "Maybe those men would be alive if you had. Should I wish that you'd never gotten involved?"

Did she think he'd enjoyed taking their lives? "You can say whatever you want. But maybe you should also know that if there were other choices, I would still make the same decisions I made today."

She looked shocked. Surprised that he would stand by his actions. The actions that had killed two men and probably began a statewide manhunt for them both. But he'd also meant making love to her, picking up the evidence cell and speaking to her at the diner.

He stared into her rich amethyst eyes and knew he'd be a happy man waking up next to them every day. Could he make that happen? Make her understand? Maybe see that he was more than a way to rescue her family?

"I get it, Bree. I'm a means to an end. Been there a lot over the years. No hard feelings." He reached into his bag of gear, tossing Larry's cell onto the seat. "We have the money. We have a phone to contact them. All we need is a car when we land and a place for the exchange."

"And a giant miracle."

"Miracles are for amateurs." The machine was back.

"Ah, folks, I think we may have a little problem." The pilot pointed to just off the runway as they landed.

Bree leaned around Jake, who had been checking his gear and keeping Dallas silent with a stern look and snap of his fingers. The snowplow had cleared a small area for planes and next to it were two police cars.

"You just had to do things your way." Waffling between fury and desperation, she could only stare through the plane windows.

"Wasn't me. Think about it. If I'd called the police, I wouldn't have fled the scene of a double homicide." He removed the gun at his waist and zipped it into the bag. "The police are normally smart, Bree. Add two and two together and they ended up with Amarillo. It's not a big leap from my truck to a plane headed here."

He was right. The desire to admit he was correct brought the words to the tip of her tongue, but she bit her lip instead. It was over. There wasn't a possibility they'd be together. Ever.

She'd failed her family.

Ernie slowed to a stop. "The tower's telling us to open the door and throw out any weapons we might have. Then exit one at a time. I'm supposed to go first, then open the rear door for you guys." He showed his empty hands in the window, opened the door next to him and got out.

Bree unhooked her seat belt, took Dallas into her arms and kissed her between the ears. "I'm going to miss you so much, you sweet little puppy."

"You'll see her again."

"I don't know how I'm going to survive in jail without pets. I've always preferred four paws to the two-legged variety." If they couldn't arrange a ransom exchange… She couldn't think of her family. She'd be a hysterical mess by the time her feet touched the ground.

"We'll convince them to help with the rescue of your family. You have enough evidence here to prosecute. We convince the police to back us up while we get names and an exchange site. It'll happen. Trust me."

"If they don't go for your idea, well, thanks anyway. For everything, Jake. My gratitude isn't nearly enough for what you've lost helping me."

The outside door opened. She shifted to the nearest seat, ready to climb down. He darted behind her, holding her elbow in spite of the no-touching rule. "It's not over. There's still a chance to free your family."

She climbed through the opening and made kissing sounds for Dallas to come to her. She looked at Jake one last time, wishing she hadn't pulled away and hoping he knew she didn't blame him.

"Thanks for trying, but it's time to give up."

She expected to be thrown to the ground, searched and hauled off to a horrible little interrogation room. She hoped not to cry or be hysterical during the entire interview, since she knew there was no hope of a rescue for her family.

Ernie was placed in a police car and driven away. Dallas was on her leash, walking in circles, looking for a place to go in the snow. Two officers held guns on her, and after a minute, Jake tossed his black bag to the ground and stood next to her, his arms folded behind his head.

Dallas whined. She didn't like the snow at all and wanted to be held. After this trip, she would be completely spoiled. "May I pick her up?"

One of the officers shrugged.

"I don't get it," Jake said. "What's going on?" Jake didn't favor his side. If she hadn't known about the laceration along his ribs, she wouldn't have been able to tell.

"We were given orders to wait."

A police car arrived and a familiar face flicked a finger at the officers to follow him. "Bring them inside."

The officers escorted them into the hangar. Officer

Wilder took the leash from her and gave it to the man who'd dropped Jake's bag at his feet. "Walk the dog, get it some water and then wait in the car, Powell."

Jake positioned himself between her and one of her former clients. He was probably as confused as she was at the strange treatment.

"When I heard the news that Sabrina Watkins's fingerprints had been found at a crime scene I spit out my coffee."

"Do you know this cop, Bree?"

"I know his wife better, but yes, this is Kyle Wilder. I used to board his dogs when his wife forced him to take a vacation."

"Detective Craig?" Kyle extended his hand. Jake let it hang in the air. "Thanks for getting Sabrina back safely. I have an officer who's going to escort you to Wichita Falls as soon as the roads are clear."

"I don't understand," Jake said along with her.

"You left two bodies and the WFPD wants a statement. Numerous witnesses stated it was self-defense. Then I think the Dallas P.D. wants to clear up the confusion regarding a suspension."

"That I get, but you're taking Bree's rising from the grave all in stride. Are you arresting her?"

Kyle raised an inquisitive eyebrow while nodding toward Jake. "Other than being wanted for questioning in the Richardson homicide, why would I detain her?"

What?

"You let her go and she'll be dead as soon as she's out of your sight." Jake placed his body between her and the officer again. "Is that your game? You the cop who switched the dental records?"

"Funny you should mention that, Detective Craig. Since the explosion last summer, I've been working with state investigators on a joint task force." He sat on the edge of a table next to the wall. "They've suspected that Griffin Tyler has been involved in racketeering and money laundering for a while, especially after Sabrina's suspicious death. We found a couple of our officers who were a little too cozy with Tyler and have our eye on them, too. If you're willing to testify, we might be able to drop any charges that apply."

"You've got the wrong—"

"Jake." She tried to tug him to face her. She took a step next to him when he refused to look anywhere but at the man he considered a threat. "I'm standing right here and very capable of speaking for myself. I'm not guilty of anything except running."

"Are you willing to cooperate?"

"I'm willing to do anything. But first, I need to find my family. Griffin is holding them hostage in exchange for money I took when I left."

"That explains a lot." He looked at Jake. "Doesn't look like the roads will be clearing anytime soon. I assume you want to see this through?"

Jake stuck his hand forward and Kyle shook it.

"Where's your task force?" Jake asked. "Once we place the call, we'll want to move quickly."

"You're looking at it. Things are a little different out here, Detective."

Jake pivoted and thrust his hand into his hair. Then his eyes locked with hers and he grabbed her shoulders. "Do you trust me?"

"Yes." And she did. If they'd been alone she would have admitted how sorry she was for thinking the worst of him. He'd defended himself and her. Anyone would have done the same.

"My idea's simple. Draw them out, see if we can't get

a confession and find out who they're working for," Jake said to the officer.

"You don't know?" Kyle asked her.

"I didn't know—"

"She wasn't—" Jake began at the same time, but her hand on his arm stopped him. She did her own questioning glance to see if he'd let her continue.

"I survived because I overheard them planning to blow up the clinic. I've tried to put things together—like a list of clients who don't exist or have never had pet surgeries. I'll turn over everything just as soon as my family's safe."

"I'd have to go through the department to obtain the equipment necessary for what you're suggesting."

Her heart stampeded. "But the officer Griffin's working with could find out and warn him."

Jake lifted his black duffel holding the money and electronics onto the workbench. "I can help with that."

Chapter Twenty-Three

They'd made the call. Bree's family was alive. And they were waiting in the pitch black fifteen miles southwest of town at an abandoned ranch for the exchange. Might as well have been on the moon for local response time. Why did criminals always have to meet in the dark? They'd waited all afternoon in the airport hangar updating Wilder, waiting on officers he could trust.

Jake didn't envy Wilder's part in the rescue. He was on foot, waist deep in snow, waiting for a signal to move in and make the arrest.

"You were right about not giving up." Bree was in the passenger seat, gripping the bag of money like a lifeline. "I know this is coming late, but I really appreciate everything you've done. We'd all be dead if you hadn't made the decision to help."

"Just follow the plan this time." He would not let his guard down. "If that lunatic hadn't insisted you be the one carrying the money, you wouldn't be here at all."

"I recognized his voice. It's the guy who was with Griffin at the clinic. I've had plenty of nightmares about him trying to kill me."

He knew all about nightmares and didn't want that for Bree. His hand covered hers without discussing it with his brain first. His brain would have reminded them that there was a no-touching policy in effect. "I'm… It'll be okay. Just follow the plan. You get to your family and run. Leave the rest to me."

He wanted to comfort her. Wanted more. His family. Her family. The whole package.

Dead Larry's phone rang.

"Yes?" Bree answered, as they'd instructed.

"That's on this road? Okay." She disconnected. "We drive to the feed lots we passed at the corner, get out and wait."

"Did you get that, Wilder?" he said, for the benefit of the transmitter he shared with the cop. He'd only had two. When Bree ran and she was out of sight, he wouldn't have contact with her.

"It'll take me ten or twelve minutes on foot," Wilder answered.

"Got it." Jake put the Jeep in gear and battled the snow-covered road. "Remember. Don't move forward until your family does. You drop the bag and get to cover."

"Got it."

"I have confidence in you, Bree." He couldn't tell her just how much. Wilder could hear everything they said. Instead, he squeezed her hand again when he pulled to a stop.

They parked and got out, waiting in front of the dark-ened vehicle.

"Wilder?" Jake whispered, barely moving his lips.

"At least five minutes away."

Three bodies turned the corner, close together as if their legs were— "They're not going to be able to run. Their legs are lashed together as if they're in a three-legged race."

"They'll run. Follow the plan," Bree said with confidence.

"Right. The only cover is in the lot with the cattle. They're tied together. You can't get them through the pipe fence, so you'll have to bring them back to the car. If something goes wrong, run up the road through the pens. Walk slow now. Run later. You've got the knife in your pocket, right?"

She looked up at him. "Should I go?"

He wanted to shout no but nodded yes. He wanted to kiss her, but she'd already opened the door and taken the first step away. Where was the "machine" when he needed him?

BREE WALKED SLOWLY, the snow crunching under her boots. She slowed even more, wanting to meet her family as close to the drive into the feed lot as she could. The wind hummed through the electrical wires high overhead. Another front was moving in from the south behind her. She could smell the cattle to her left, hear them moving toward the fence where they expected to be fed.

"That's far enough." A shout came from somewhere behind the buildings. It was the voice she'd never forget.

Her family stopped. She stopped and dropped the bag at her side. She'd soon be face-to-face with her nightmare.

"Open the bag."

She unzipped the duffel and a spotlight shone on her from the top of a grain silo. She left the bag in the snow. "Here's half. I want my family back."

"You were supposed to bring me all the money."

"And you'll get it if you just let them go."

"Sabrina Watkins." The voice was closer, in the direct path of where she intended to run. "You and your boyfriend have cost us a lot of time and money. Our entire operation here is…kaput."

She saw the outline of a gun in his hand as he walked toward her. Kyle had told them Larry had a brother. She could see the resemblance, especially in their horrible, evil eyes.

"Stay back, boyfriend," he shouted. "I think we'll do this the hard but fun way. Pick up the money and walk to me."

"What?" This wasn't the plan. How could she get her family out of here if she was with him? But Jake was there. He could get her family out.

Waving his gun like a flag, he stomped the ground. "Sit!" he screamed, and pointed at her family. They tumbled into the muddy snow, tied like they were. "See, dog trainer? I'm a good trainer, too. They obey or the punishment is my partner shoots. Now pick up the money and come with me."

"No! That's not the deal," Jake shouted. "The rest of the money's hidden. We'll tell Tyler where to pick it up."

"Tyler's dead. He can't find anything." He waved over his shoulder, pointing to Jake. "I think your boyfriend likes you."

Three quick shots were fired. "Son of a b—" Jake dove to the far side of the Jeep.

"Pick up the money, Sabrina."

"You'll leave my family alone?"

"Maybe." He raised the opposite hand into the air. Her family cringed. Her father covered her sister as best he could with his body.

"All right. I can take you to the rest of the money." All she had to do was make it into the cattle lot. They couldn't shoot her family if they were trying to shoot her. She picked up the bag and looped it over her shoulder.

Her nightmare lifted his arm, attempting to grab her. She sidestepped, scooting through the snow and getting a couple of steps ahead of him. "Let them walk to the Jeep."

"Sure."

They stood as she got even with the cattle. Thank goodness, her father encouraged them to shuffle faster. She walked backward, watching her family and staying more than a lunge away from their captor.

They were very close to Jake by the time she was at the gate.

RUN! JAKE'S FIST hit his leg again and again. He pulled his knife from his boot, ready to cut the ropes and get Bree's family to safety. He inched around the fender, trying to spot the man who'd fired at him.

"Wilder, from the angle of those shots, cover the top of the silo." Bree was at the gate and out of time. *Run!*

"I'm crossing the south pen. Damn snowdrifts and manure."

"I'm sending the family out in the Jeep and following Bree."

"Roger," Wilder acknowledged. "There's a truck headed in from the north."

"I didn't think it would be easy. I'll get the family. You get the shooter." Jake had his knife in hand and sprinted the remaining ten or so feet to Bree's family.

Rifle shots echoed. "He's either a lousy shot or—"

"Bree made a break. She didn't get away from him…." Wilder trailed off.

Jake had to focus on one rescue at a time. Get the family out. Think of nothing else or he was useless. A shot hit the Jeep. The shooter would correct his aim soon.

"Pick up your daughter and keep running as best you can. I'll carry your wife."

Jake didn't have time to verify if Watkins understood or not. They all kept running. He met them, cut their ropes and lifted Bree's mother off the ground by her waist, very glad she was about the same size as both her daughters.

He had the three of them on the safe side of the Jeep before he cut and removed their ropes completely.

Jake yanked out his bag of gear and pushed Bree's sister into the back of the Jeep. "Stay low. Drive. Don't stop. Don't look back. We'll meet you at the police station. Address is in the GPS."

"Is Sabrina really alive?" asked Bree's mother. "Was that really her?"

"Yes, ma'am. Sorry, I can't explain."

"Thank you," Watkins said, and began backing down the road as a truck sped into view and gunned its engine.

"Anytime now, Wilder. Anytime." Jake picked up his rifle and ran to the cattle fence. It was the only cover he had and that might make it harder for the shooter to actually hit him.

"I think I have the shooter. I warned you about my marksmanship."

"I'm taking out the truck so they can't follow the family. Cover me if nothing else."

Jake sprinted along the path he'd cleared to the road as the truck gained speed to follow the Watkins family. He dug deep, blew out his breath and fired at the front tires until he heard the blowout and the truck swerved into the far barbed-wire fence.

"Do you have eyes on Bree?" he shouted over the continuing gunfire behind him.

"Negative. There you are, you son of—" A lone rifle shot, then another, then something fell and clanked against the metal of the silo. "Done. My team's in place around the perimeter. They can't get out of the lot."

Jake left the men in the truck—alive, dead or unconscious, he didn't care. Wilder could take care of them. "I'm heading after Bree."

Chapter Twenty-Four

"Shut up and keep moving."

"Which direction?" Bree asked.

The man she'd been so petrified of for six months, who had haunted her dreams on a regular basis, shoved between her shoulder blades and cursed when she fell.

He grabbed her coat and hauled her back to her feet. "Fall again, bitch, and I might as well blow your head off."

"Tell me which way to go and I won't fall." For once she didn't cower. Afraid, definitely. And she had no idea if anyone was following to help her out of this mess. But she knew the police were out there. This monster wouldn't get free to haunt someone else. There was still a chance she could survive. She just had to figure out how.

With the faint yellow glow of the mercury lights, they followed the road used to load and feed the cattle. There were tire tracks from earlier in the day that were quickly getting slick without the sun to melt the snow.

Thinking they would be fed again, the cattle pushed toward the fence, jumping on one another's backs, bucking, mooing.

"Cut across that pen to the left."

This was her chance. She could go through the pipe fence, but her abductor would have to climb over. She'd have precious seconds to disappear among the cattle. She followed his instructions, sliding through the icy pipes, pushing her way through the cattle as fast as they'd move out of her way.

"I swear, girl, if you make another move, I'll shoot you through the head," he said, perched on the top row.

She stopped as best she could with the cows pressing against her. Even if the man fired and missed, she'd be crushed between these huge animals. He entered the pen and shoved his way to her side, sticking the gun against her temple.

"You might not care much about your own hide, but think about your family and friends. I *will* get out of here and I *will* slice all their throats." He shoved her head and then shoved the cows.

The cows squeezed her between them, crushed her toes and clamored to get closer. Crossing the pen was exhausting and disgusting in the slush and manure. They were at the mercy of which way the cattle swayed for the longest time. Then the herd sort of turned the opposite direction. Maybe...

A long shadow fell across the backs of the cows. Someone was cutting across the pens on top of the fence. She pointed to the opposite corner and said, "That way's open."

Very few cows were between her and the field where they'd been heading. She picked up her pace, hoping whoever followed could get to her soon. *Please, please, please, let it be Jake.*

"What are you looking at?"

Her nightmare spun to look behind them and she ran. Something hit her back and tangled her feet, tripping her. She caught a glimpse of Jake at the side of the pen where they were headed.

"Drop your weapon, Leroy. Don't move and stay where

you are." Jake's voice shouted across the pen. "Lot seventy-seven, come in silent."

Would Leroy know he was telling the police where they were?

"Or you'll shoot? Your girlfriend's on the ground, Detective. Spook a cow and she's dead." His boot went square on her stomach, keeping her pinned down in the icy mud.

Her feet were untangled, but Leroy had his gun pointed at her. They were in a corner with fewer cows, but he was right. One little spook and she'd be trampled.

"I think it's your turn to drop your weapon."

"You got nowhere to go, man. The police will have this place surrounded in a matter of minutes."

The cattle had noticed Jake at the rail. They'd all be clamoring on top of each other soon. She pushed at Leroy's boot, desperate to get off the ground. *How?* She couldn't see Jake and her knife had been taken away from her back at the first gate.

What had her self-defense instructor told them to do if caught on the ground? Pull the attacker's clothes to get them off balance. She began tugging at his jeans, then rocking her body back and forth. As soon as his foot shifted, she twisted from under him and rolled to the other side of a cow.

"I'm free, Jake!"

Someone fired. She scrambled to her knees and headed away in the direction of the fewest cattle. She found an open spot, stood and pushed between anxious cows heading in all directions because of the gunfire.

And anxious because of a fight. She climbed to the top of the fence in time to see Jake land two good punches to the other man's jaw. He stumbled backward, but Jake stayed on top of him. With a punch to his gut, the man fell against a large white cow and that evil grin she'd seen at the clinic slithered onto his face. It seemed like a lifetime ago but she recognized it.

"He's got my knife!"

She watched a repeat of this morning's fight with that young kid. Every slash of the blade was perfectly countered by Jake. His arm dripped blood from a gash but he didn't slow down. And then the move that had killed that crazy young man in Wichita Falls was repeated.

This man fell, crazed eyes squinting shut, never crying out. Jake dropped to his knees and Bree jumped from the fence to run to his side.

"Oh, God, Jake. Are you all right?" Her voice was low and scared.

They made it safely to and over the fence in time to watch several police cars sloshing through the snow. They sat on the curb of the feed trough, waiting. The cattle followed to the fence behind them, noisy and wanting to be fed. They seemed unaffected by the fight.

Totally unlike her.

"You're bleeding. Is Kyle still listening to you through the microphone?"

"I lost the earpiece after the first punch to my face. It's somewhere out in the muck." Jake shook off her hands from his arms. "God, I thought he'd shot you. Thought you were dead." He gently trapped her face with his long fingers and she covered his hands, keeping him close. "I'm not sure where this relationship will lead, Bree. But I don't want it to end."

"This is crazy, Jake. We met yesterday morning. You don't have to say that because we had an interlude."

"You what?" Kyle Wilder asked as he walked up. "Are you about to kiss that witness, Detective Craig?"

They split apart. An officer brought a first-aid kit to look at Jake's arm and Kyle backed her out of the way. "It will complicate my case if you're having a fling with the detective."

"We barely know each other." She didn't believe that. They'd connected somehow. Or was it just extenuating circumstances?

"Good, because a relationship with a suspect would just be another bad mark in his file." Kyle had lowered his voice so the other officers couldn't hear.

"To think we have a relationship is stupid. I just met him yesterday." It didn't matter if she felt something or not. After everything Jake had done for her, she wasn't going to let him get into trouble for kissing her—or sleeping with her.

Kyle guided her down the road to a car ready to pull out. "Get in, Sabrina." When she hesitated, his grip on her arm prevented her from running back to Jake. "I'm not asking."

"Why are they arresting him? You said—" She twisted free and took a step toward the officers escorting Jake to another police car. "Are we both under arrest?"

Kyle caught her arm again and snapped a cuff around her wrist. "I've been instructed to get you into protective custody and out of Amarillo. You're the key to bringing these scumbags to justice. Now get in the car."

She wanted to explain to Jake how she felt. "Can't I see him for a minute?"

"We have to obtain your statements separately. I can't let you see your parents, either."

"I...I don't understand, Kyle."

"This money-laundering scam is huge and you're the key to putting them in jail. They're cleaning house. My men found Griffin Tyler shot through the head in his home. They've been trying to kill you for six months. Do you think they're stopping now?"

"What if I refuse? I mean, Jake's done a fantastic job of protecting me and—"

"Will he be able to protect all your family? What if he does jail time for his actions at his precinct?"

"If I go with you he'll be cleared?"

Kyle nodded. She got in the car and he closed the door.

Police protection scared her more than when she'd been held at knifepoint by Larry. She rubbed the place on her neck where the blade had cut her. But why? She had no reason not to trust Kyle. What worried her was not seeing her family.

And not telling Jake how much he meant to her. Maybe she hadn't answered him, but she could clear his name and guarantee that he got his old job back. She could do that much for the marine who'd defended her so completely.

JAKE DIDN'T LIKE sitting in the backseat of a police cruiser. Locked on the wrong side of the glass, he could only watch as Kyle Wilder drove Bree away from the scene. An officer took him to the station and put him in an interview room. He had a lot of explaining to do to his captain, the Wichita Falls police and, right now, to a special task force rep in a nice, clean suit.

Jake still stunk from rolling in the feed lots. The only thing clean on him was the bandage where they'd dressed the knife wound on his arm.

"Detective Craig, the state of Texas would like to thank you for your help. I'm going to get your statement and make arrangements for your travel back to DFW." He set a pad and pencil on the table.

Jake stood and leaned on the table, looking down on whatever officer was attempting to be nice to him. "Where's Sabrina Watkins?"

"Miss Watkins is no longer in Amarillo. She's been secured."

Secured? "When can I see her?" Jake sat, trying to keep a lid on the fury coursing through him.

"I have no information. Nor, if I did, would I be able to share it with you, Detective."

"So where's my dog?"

"Pardon?"

Jake knew the drill. He'd done it too many times himself. They wanted his recollections as fast as he could get them written. He pushed the notepad an arm's length away.

"Kyle Wilder sent my pup, Dallas, with an officer when we landed at the airport. She could be at the pound for all I know. And that's not going to happen. I'll make my statement when you find my dog." Bree's dog that he'd keep until she said otherwise. He laced his fingers behind his head. The tape on his side pinched his skin, but he kept a straight face. "Don't shake your head and tell me I'm not in a position to make demands. Come on, man. Just find my dog and get me a hamburger. I'm starved."

The officer scooped up the pen and paper and left. Ten minutes later, Dallas bounded through the door.

"There's my girl." *At least one of them.*

When the time was right, he'd demand to see Bree. And if he couldn't—if he could hang on to the pup, he was certain they'd find each other sooner or later.

Chapter Twenty-Five

The jumping Chihuahua in Bree's stomach had twenty pals join him. Testifying had nothing on the nerves she was trying to get under control. Facing Jake after five long, lonely months waiting to testify might be harder than walking that snow-covered road with a gun to her head. That night she'd known Jake would come after her. Today, she had no way of predicting how he'd react to her just showing up.

This house with the rolling hill country backdrop was a far cry from Jake's one-bedroom apartment.

"So, this is the place. I'll wait for you if you want," Mr. Soku, the driver, said with a foreign accent.

She'd had plenty of time to share her doubts about arriving unannounced. Her fear had just come pouring out to her driver.

"I can't do this, after all. Can you turn—" A bark and familiar howl stopped her. *Dallas*. She didn't even need to see the puppy to know who beckoned to her. "I'll call when I'm ready to go. It might be as soon as five minutes."

"I'll be close by, Miss Sabrina. Much good fortune to you. I wish you luck finding your happy beginning."

"Thank you so very much, Mr. Soku." She paid him and got out the driver's side door he opened, standing in the deserted street as he drove away.

Dallas barked from behind the fence. Mr. Soku honked

from the corner, leaning out his window and gesturing that she move from her spot. She couldn't or was afraid to take a step. What if Jake rejected her? A vehicle turned the corner and she had to get out of its way. There wasn't a sidewalk so she quickly walked down the driveway to the porch.

A door slammed and she wanted to look behind her, but that petrified feeling had her glued, facing the bell. If she turned away, she'd keep right on walking. *Chicken*. She pushed the doorbell and waited. There was scratching at the door, more barking and a bit of howling.

"May I help you, ma'am?" asked a deep, sexy voice from behind her.

Jumping Chihuahuas, she'd missed that voice. It started all sorts of bubbly good things inside her.

"Hi, Jake." She turned to greet him, hand extended, hoping he'd smile and not turn her away. Could she run in this tight sundress and heels to catch Mr. Soku? Had it been five minutes?

The tall marine-turned-homicide-detective-turned-state-investigator gulped. He gulped again and looked around as if he was embarrassed to have her on his steps, let alone near his house. "I didn't recognize you as a blonde and in that— That's some dress, Bree. What are you doing here?"

"Oh, no. I'm sorry. I should have called." She darted down the single step, hearing the little howl behind the door. It broke her heart as much as the confused look on Jake's face.

His hand darted out, catching her bare upper arm. It was blazing hot outside and just a couple of minutes in the afternoon sun had her skin heated. But Jake's touch shot a flame through every inch of her being.

"Wait. They told me you were coming to see Dallas."

She had come a very long way to see *Jake*. Months of wondering and debating. She stepped back under the shade of the porch and searched his dark eyes. "You look great, Jake."

As soon as he got through the door, he ignored Dallas until she sat in front of him. "Good girl. You ready to eat?" The dog was twice the size she'd been five months earlier. All legs, she bounded to Bree before chasing around the corner, sliding on the wooden floors after Jake.

Bree stayed in the entry hall, unsure about where to go and completely convinced this had been the wrong thing to do. They'd known each other for less than two full days. He'd moved on with his life while hers had been in limbo waiting in protective custody.

Jake stuck his head around the corner. "Coming?"

"Your home's very beautiful."

"I got a good deal on it. The owners were downsizing and left a lot of the furnishings, and Dallas needed a yard." He scooped dog food into a dish. "Come on, girl. You know the drill. Sit."

The Lab plopped down, her long tail sweeping the floor as it wagged behind her.

"You're so good together. I'm glad you decided to keep her."

Jake's face scrunched up in confusion. "You thought I'd give her away?"

"No." She shook her head. She wanted a do-over. Maybe if she ran back to the front door and he answered it, she could get the speech out she'd practiced all morning on the plane. Jake gave Dallas one last stroke and stood, making Bree crane her neck to look him in the eye. "I'd forgotten just how tall you were. You all healed?"

Her dress spun with her as she turned to go. She'd never come back. Never see him again. She couldn't do this more than once. She remembered the slick new heels just as her feet slipped from under her and she fell into Jake's arms. He set her in the kitchen chair faster than she'd thought possible. In a matter of seconds, he faced her from across the table and quirked an eyebrow in her direction.

The warrior who had risked everything to help her and rescue her family materialized as he tossed an envelope onto the table. "I got the papers. You're suing for joint custody of Dallas? You came to take away my dog?"

"What? I didn't—I was joking when I said I might. I'd never take her away from you, Jake. You're right. She's your dog now." She loved the puppy who had brought them together, but she loved Jake more. "I never had any intention of taking her away. I had this weird conversation with an attorney, but I didn't go through with it. I was going to use the story as an icebreaker...not a deal breaker."

"So it was a joke?"

"They shouldn't have done anything at all."

"That's different, then. You know, I can let you have as much time with Dallas as you want. Anytime you're in town." He stuck his hands in his pockets, shoulders sort of drooping.

She stood, swaying in the stupid, sexy shoes she'd worn just for him. She kicked them to the side and bent down next to the dog.

Dallas nudged her snout under Bree's hand, looking for some loving. Suddenly, it was like they hadn't been apart. If only finding love was that simple.

"I really came here to tell you I was wrong."

"About?" He shot a hand through his hair and brought it back to scratch the stubble on his jawline.

She grabbed the edge of the table, knowing what would come next—a surge of longing for him. That simple gesture just made her weak in the knees. "Shoot, Jake. There's no tippy-toeing around why I came. I wanted to see you. I missed you."

"And Dallas, don't forget." He was teasing her. The twinkle was back in his eyes.

"I missed you both. I wanted to call more than once, but the prosecutors wouldn't let me."

"I didn't know how hard to push. The last time we were together you told Wilder we didn't know each other. That to think we had a relationship was stupid—your words, not mine. And to think we had more than a one-night stand— also your words—was completely foolish."

"I told him that so you wouldn't get into any more trouble. I was also very wrong. Our two days together got me through the last five months."

Jake's fingers brushed a tear from her cheek and he shifted her into the circle of his arms. He heated her core and sent shivers up her spine at the same time. No man had ever made her feel anything close to these sensations. His lips were close and just waiting...so she kissed him. He tasted cool, like iced tea and lemon. His arms circled her back and pulled her close to his chest.

Dallas whined and jumped on them both, making it impossible to kiss through their laughter. "No need to be jealous, girl." Bree stroked the black, wiry fur.

"I wanted to turn you around and do that from the moment I saw you in the street," he said into her hair.

"I thought you didn't recognize me?"

He latched those brown eyes to hers. "I'd be able to pick you out of a crowd at a hundred yards. I couldn't believe you were finally here."

Jake shrugged out of his coat as he dialed his cell. "I need to send a text canceling tonight. You see, this crazy chick I knew suggested I get therapy."

"I did not. I just said working with Charlie helped my uncle."

"It didn't take me long to realize how much Dallas was helping me deal with stress. I found an organization that helps military vets find the right pet and I volunteer."

He faced her and pushed his hands through his hair. A sure sign that he was nervous regarding whatever he was about to say. She barely knew him, but then she also knew him so well.

"Bree, the time I spent with you—" He took her hand into his palm, using his thumb to draw those concentric circles that drove her mad with desire. "They were the best hours of my life. I've missed you every minute since."

He tipped her chin and tilted her world with his smile.

"You're crying again and I haven't even gotten to the good part," he whispered near her lips.

Sure enough, tears leaked out of the corners of her eyes. "There's a better part?"

"I know it's early and I'll give you all the time you need. But I fell all the way when you ran into my life. Being apart has only convinced me that I love you."

His lips descended and captured hers. Captured and wouldn't release. He wrapped his arms tight and held her as tenderly as their first kiss. He taunted and kept their lips devouring each other until Dallas jumped on them again.

"Definitely the best part." She leaned her cheek against his chest. "That's what I came to tell you. I love you. I thought I was crazy. I kept telling myself it couldn't be real. It was too soon. Or just one of those whirlwind adventures. Maybe a bond I felt because of the intense situation."

"Me, too." He hugged her to him, keeping her close, his breath tickled her neck. "I kept thinking we'd see each other somewhere throughout all this process. But the police kept us separated in Amarillo and then the state authorities threatened me within an inch of my life not to compromise the case again. They offered me a position with the Texas Racing Commission. I couldn't turn them down."

"I wanted to call so badly. Kyle Wilder assured me they'd give me your address after I testified. The prosecution placed me in protective custody, locking me in a safe house in the middle of nowhere. It made Amarillo look like a metropolitan city. I've had a lot of time to think. But my feelings about you haven't changed."

"The state prosecutor kept telling me I couldn't see you. And when I called your uncle last month—"

"You talked to Jerry?"

"Yeah, but he didn't know where you were. Said the family got one letter, but had no idea what was really going on."

"One letter with no real details was all they'd allow."

"No one could have convinced me I'd fall this hard or fast. Or that I'd start missing you before we said goodbye. But I did...." His voice trailed off as he nibbled on her neck. "I hope you're staying for a while. Maybe a week or two? I warned them I'd be taking off as soon as I knew where you were."

His burning lips left a smoldering trail across her collarbone. She pulled back to see his eyes reflecting the desire she felt.

"As for your petition for custody." He paused to kiss her, leaving a burning trail from the backs of his fingers running along her exposed skin. "If you want to spend time with Dallas, we're a package deal. You're stuck with the both of us. Move in with me."

He lifted her, twirling her through the kitchen, laughing and playfully taunting Dallas.

"Sounds like perfect joint custody." She kissed his furrowed brow that she'd missed every day. "Remind me to call Mr. Soku at the cab company. He wished me luck finding my happy beginning. I want to tell him it worked."

* * * * *

COMING NEXT MONTH FROM

◆ HARLEQUIN®

INTRIGUE®

Available January 21, 2014

#1473 BLOOD ON COPPERHEAD TRAIL
Bitterwood P.D.
Paula Graves

Laney Hanvey's job fighting corruption pits her against police chief
Doyle Massey, but they must work together when three girls disappear.

#1474 UNDERCOVER CAPTOR
Shadow Agents: Guts and Glory
Cynthia Eden

When Dr. Tina Jamison is kidnapped by a group determined to destroy
the EOD, her only hope of survival rests with dangerous undercover agent
Drew Lancaster.

#1475 ROCKY MOUNTAIN REVENGE
Cindi Myers

FBI agent Jacob Westmoreland tracks down his former flame,
Elizabeth Giardino, in order to bring one man to justice: her father.

#1476 TENNESSEE TAKEDOWN
Lena Diaz

Caught at the wrong place at the wrong time, an accountant must rely
upon a hunky SWAT detective as she runs for her life.

#1477 RANCHER RESCUE
Barb Han

A cowboy comes to Katherine Harper's aid only to find himself the new
target of a man who will stop at nothing to silence them both.

#1478 RAVEN'S HOLLOW
Jenna Ryan

Eli Blume and Sadie Bellam meet again in a haunted hollow,
where someone hungering for revenge lurks in the shadows.

**YOU CAN FIND MORE INFORMATION ON UPCOMING HARLEQUIN® TITLES,
FREE EXCERPTS AND MORE AT WWW.HARLEQUIN.COM.**

HICNM0114

REQUEST YOUR FREE BOOKS!
2 FREE NOVELS PLUS 2 FREE GIFTS!

H HARLEQUIN®

INTRIGUE®

BREATHTAKING ROMANTIC SUSPENSE

YES! Please send me 2 FREE Harlequin Intrigue® novels and my 2 FREE gifts (gifts are worth about $10). After receiving them, if I don't wish to receive any more books, I can return the shipping statement marked "cancel." If I don't cancel, I will receive 6 brand-new novels every month and be billed just $4.74 per book in the U.S. or $5.24 per book in Canada. That's a savings of at least 14% off the cover price! It's quite a bargain! Shipping and handling is just 50¢ per book in the U.S. and 75¢ per book in Canada.* I understand that accepting the 2 free books and gifts places me under no obligation to buy anything. I can always return a shipment and cancel at any time. Even if I never buy another book, the two free books and gifts are mine to keep forever.

182/382 HDN F42N

Name _____ (PLEASE PRINT) _____

Address _____ Apt. # _____

City _____ State/Prov. _____ Zip/Postal Code _____

Signature (if under 18, a parent or guardian must sign)

Mail to the **Harlequin® Reader Service:**
IN U.S.A.: P.O. Box 1867, Buffalo, NY 14240-1867
IN CANADA: P.O. Box 609, Fort Erie, Ontario L2A 5X3
**Are you a subscriber to Harlequin Intrigue books
and want to receive the larger-print edition?
Call 1-800-873-8635 or visit www.ReaderService.com.**

* Terms and prices subject to change without notice. Prices do not include applicable taxes. Sales tax applicable in N.Y. Canadian residents will be charged applicable taxes. Offer not valid in Quebec. This offer is limited to one order per household. Not valid for current subscribers to Harlequin Intrigue books. All orders subject to credit approval. Credit or debit balances in a customer's account(s) may be offset by any other outstanding balance owed by or to the customer. Please allow 4 to 6 weeks for delivery. Offer available while quantities last.

Your Privacy—The Harlequin® Reader Service is committed to protecting your privacy. Our Privacy Policy is available online at www.ReaderService.com or upon request from the Harlequin Reader Service.

We make a portion of our mailing list available to reputable third parties that offer products we believe may interest you. If you prefer that we not exchange your name with third parties, or if you wish to clarify or modify your communication preferences, please visit us at www.ReaderService.com/consumerschoice or write to us at Harlequin Reader Service Preference Service, P.O. Box 9062, Buffalo, NY 14269. Include your complete name and address.

HI13R

BLOOD ON COPPERHEAD TRAIL
by Paula Graves

Nothing can stop Laney Hanvey from looking for her missing
sister. Not even sexy new chief of Bitterwood P.D....

"I'm not going to be handled out of looking for my sister,"
Laney growled as she heard footsteps catching up behind
her on the hiking trail.

"I'm just here to help."

She faltered to a stop, turning to look at Doyle Massey.
He wasn't exactly struggling to keep up with her—life on the
beach had clearly kept him in pretty good shape. But he was
out of his element.

She'd grown up in these mountains. Her mother had
always joked she was half mountain goat, half Indian scout.
She knew these hills as well as she knew her own soul. "You'll
slow me down."

"Maybe that's a good thing."

She glared at him, her rising terror looking for a target.
"My sister is out here somewhere and I'm going to find her."

The look Doyle gave her was full of pity. The urge to slap
that expression off his face was so strong she had to clench her
hands. "You're rushing off alone into the woods where a man
with a gun has just committed a murder."

"A gun?" She couldn't stop her gaze from slanting toward
the crime scene. "She was shot?"

"Two rounds to the back of the head."

She closed her eyes, the remains of the cucumber sandwich she'd eaten at Sequoyah House rising in her throat. She stumbled a few feet away from Doyle Massey and gave up fighting the nausea.

After her stomach was empty, she crouched in the underbrush, fighting dry heaves and giving in to the hot tears burning her eyes. The heat of Massey's hand on her back was comforting, even though she was embarrassed by her display.

"I will help you search," he said in a low, gentle tone. "But I want you to take a minute to just breathe and think. Okay? I want you to think about your sister and where you think she'd go. Do you know?"

Does Laney hold the key to her sister's whereabouts?
Doyle Massey intends to find out, in Paula Graves's
BLOOD ON COPPERHEAD TRAIL,
on sale in February 2014!

INTRIGUE

BROKEN HEARTS OUTLAST BROKEN BONES

It can't be a coincidence. In the past twenty-four hours, three different thugs have tried to kill or abduct Ashley Parish. Sexy SWAT team leader Dillon Gray saved her, but now he wonders why someone would want to murder the beautiful accountant…and why he finds her so infuriatingly attractive! After being hurt in love, all Dillon can handle are heart-sparing one-night stands.

But once the FBI comes after Ashley for embezzlement, Dillon knows he must protect her from a killer—and prove she's being framed. Taking her on a hair-raising run through dangerous terrain doesn't daunt the fearless hero…but wanting her for more than one night does.

TENNESSEE TAKEDOWN

BY LENA DIAZ

Available February 2014, only from Harlequin® Intrigue®.